SECOND CHANCE RANCH

Books by Audra Harders

From Love Inspired Books:
Rocky Mountain Hero

For eBook:

Circle D series:
Second Chance Ranch
Rough Road Home
Her Christmas Cowboy, a Christmas novella in the
Hope For The Holidays Contemporary Collection

Paperback:

Circle D series:
Second Chance Ranch
Rough Road Home

The Circle D #1

SECOND CHANCE RANCH

Audra Harders

Bible verse references from:
New King James Version

Paperback ISBN: 978-0-9960187-1-5

To my wonderful hero husband, Gary, who always encouraged me to follow my heart. God blessed me with the best when he brought you into my life.

Acknowledgments:

Any work of fiction is a collaborative effort and I thank all those who collaborated with me even when you weren't in the mood. Any errors in this work of fictions are completely owned by the author.

To **Kara Harders** who answered so many of my clueless questions about farming and equipment. You didn't roll your eyes too much when I asked about crops and rotations. Thanks for letting me pester you. You'll always be my favorite daughter.

To **Leslie Ann Sartor**, my best friend and feedback buddy. I love every moment of our road trips and retreats where we spend days tossing ideas back and forth until we've assembled characters and plots worthy to be called books.

To **Jan Warren Harders** who never batted an eye when I asked her questions about cancer, transplants and treatments. Thanks for sharing your many years of nursing oncology patients and for going to the on staff transplant team for questions beyond your comfort zone. You have a heart as big as the shadow you cast. I'll never say it enough -- welcome to the family.

To **Amanda, Julie, Mary and Ruthy** who gave unselfishly of their time to help me with conflict and plot issues. This book would not be as strong today if you hadn't taken time away from your own writing to offer suggestions and shower kudos. You guys are the best!

To *The Seekers*, my best support system ever! I thank God every day He brought us together.

To my Lord and Savior, Jesus Christ for blessing me with the desire to write. May my stories always make You smile.

"For I know the plans I have for you," says the Lord. "They are plans for good and not for disaster, to give you a future and a hope. In those days when you pray, I will listen. If you look for Me in earnest, you will find Me when you seek Me." Jeremiah 29:11-13

« CHAPTER ONE »

A THROATY CRY REVERBERATED through the dense pine trees.

Zac Davidson jerked back from the gas-operated rake in the equipment barn and squinted toward the massive log house across the dirt parking lot. The shadow of a red-tailed hawk swept across the ground. Known for its raptor habitat, the mountainous forest on the Trails' End Ranch provided a grand playground for birds of all sorts attracting wildlife to the Trails' End Ranch year long. The remote grandeur surrounding the ranch houses and outbuildings contrasted sharply with the two thousand fertile acres of hay that comprised the rest of the property directly across the Highland Creek. Zac loved it here. Though his family owned the Circle D Ranch a couple of miles away, his heart had always belonged to the Trails' End, and with patience, it would soon belong to him.

Another scream filled the air, this time from the back of the log house. Dropping the side panel of the rake, he sprinted across the lot, his boots kicking gravel along the well-worn path around the parked vehicles. He followed the rough board porch that wrapped around the house. The back door stood open as cool air from a fan blew out. An ocean tide of water covered the floor of the country-style kitchen.

"Patrick, I'm glad you came." Feminine frustration bounced off the pine cabinets. "I can't shield the water and turn off the main line under the sink at the same time."

Jennifer O'Reilly stood beside the kitchen sink, every tall, slender inch of her a soaking mess. Eyes squeezed shut, she held a roasting pan over the faucet to divert spewing water into the sink. Her long, wet hair hung down her back and across her face. Every doubt he might have had about returning home vanished with the memories of what he'd left behind so many years ago.

Nudging her aside, Zac shouldered his way under the sink. He'd correct her assumption of which shining knight had come to her rescue later. Right now, water poured from another leak in the goose-neck pipe creating a lake the size of Blue Mesa Reservoir. He grabbed the water shut-off, turning it tightly.

Water still dripped from the pipe, but from the silence up top, he'd say he'd accomplished his task. "You okay?"

"Better now." The pan dropped to the floor as her legs shifted beside him. "Didn't have time to read the fix-it manual."

Zac wormed out from under the sink and pulled himself up. Jen had a towel pressed to her eyes. She scrubbed it up over her hair and caught sight of him. A moment passed before recognition dawned.

"Hey, Bean. When did you turn plumber?" The familiar nickname just rolled off his tongue. "Thought the medical world needed soft hearts like you in the hospital, not under a sink."

Her eyes widened then returned to normal as she wrung water from her hair. "Nothing wrong with developing a few domestic skills." She brushed the towel over her shirt and sleeves. "What are you doing here? When did you get into town?"

He ignored the cool welcome and tugged her toward him. Their soaked shirts plastered together as her fingers ran across his back out of habit, inspecting him for injury. Since they were kids, Jen displayed her father's astuteness for assessing him for injury. Usually scrapes and bruises, and most times, her instincts were spot on.

Right now, he thought not of injury nor the girl, but more the soul mates they'd been in high school. Zac enveloped her in his embrace and as she turned to protest, he claimed her lips in a kiss as if his teenage years hadn't passed. Her lips molded into place with just as much eagerness. He could handle welcome homes like this all day long. Before his latent teenage urges took complete control, he pulled away and grinned at her startled frown. "Pulled into town this morning. Thought I'd see if Hawk Ridge was ready for Zac Davidson to come home. I guess it is."

"You're home? For how long this time?" She leaned back until a wedge of air separated them, her bright blue gaze searching his face. A quick shake of her head sent a strand of hair whipping across her cheek. "Nevermind. Why stop here? Jess Eklund's not here. Hasn't been for years."

"Heard you were up here and thought I'd stop by before heading to the Circle D." He studied the pipe grease about her knuckles and smeared across her shirt. "Told ya I'd always be there when you needed me."

The temperature dropped in the room. A squint of suspicion took the place of greeting as her fingers dug into his biceps and she grew still. "Zac, I'm glad whatever you have going on in Hawk Ridge brought you by the ranch today. I couldn't have stopped the deluge without you."

"You'd have gotten along fine like always." The soaked blue paisley western shirt she wore layered over an equally soaked tee clung to her womanly curves. Tucked into the waistband of her Cruel Girl jeans, the shirts bunched as she pushed damp strands from her face with one hand. Despite the unexplained brush-off, he couldn't help but appreciate the beautiful cowgirl she'd grown into.

"Probably." She nodded, the muscles in her delicate jaw worked. "Drop in on a whim and leave with a flash. Just like always."

Her cynical note issued a challenge. "That's not true."

"Remember the wedding?"

"Gabe's wedding? Of course I do. We had a blast."

She dropped her hold of him and stepped back, the tips of her toes peeking out from under her boot-cut jeans as puddles splashed all around. "You were here for two weeks before the wedding, you made me believe you missed the ol' town and all your friends.

You said you thought it was about time you came home." Her eyes flashed as she took a breath. Her knuckles turned white as she gripped the edge of the countertop, agitation pumping steam through her system. "I told you I didn't want to go to the wedding as your date. I told you people would take it the wrong way. I told you the town would talk."

Her voice caught as her shoulders squared and all the fight came to a head. "They sure got to talking when you left the next morning without saying goodbye."

He'd escorted the prettiest girl in town, besides his sister-in-law, of course. They'd danced and laughed all night. He'd felt a part of something special and the feeling had nothing to do with the joy of his brother's wedding. He'd stayed at the wedding longer than he should have, but he just couldn't leave. Because of Jen, he hadn't felt the ever present censure of the town, tolerated the disapproving looks from people with long memories, felt like apologizing for every misdeed he'd ever committed.

Because of Jennifer O'Reilly, he'd felt like one of the family rather than the black sheep, the same stigma that had sent him running from Hawk Ridge years ago. "I told you I had to go to the Cattlemen's Conference. I didn't even go to bed that night. I barely made it to registration as it was."

She locked her arms across her chest and gave him the single raised brow. "Zac, who are you kidding? You'll never call Hawk Ridge home. Now, if you'll excuse me, I have a lake to mop up before I'm due at the clinic."

He wasn't going to push it. He had some serious talking to do with Jennifer O'Reilly over a matter of equal importance to both of them. The last thing he wanted was her locked and loaded for bear. "Where's a mop? I'll help you clean up."

She turned aside and rubbed her forehead with the tips of her fingers. "I'll take care of it. Just go."

Zac wanted to argue, but thought better of it. If she wanted him gone now, fine. He'd be back. "Glad I could help with the leak. See ya soon, Bean."

ⓐ

Bean. Stupid nickname.

Jen finished mopping up the floor and tossed the last dry towel she had into the laundry pile. The dark pine floor showed every wet footstep on her way to the bathroom. Dropping her soaked clothes in a heap, she slipped into her bath robe, mumbling the whole time. Zac had this power over her since they were kids. He'd say let's go do this, and she'd follow despite her better judgment. Zac had always been a magnet for trouble. Not that he ever meant any of it, he just got carried away having a good time and left his good sense packed away until after the damage was done.

Pulling out a clean pair of jeans and a tank top, she rummaged through her closet for a shirt before facing her reflection in the mirror. What was wrong with her? Every time Zac Davidson poked his nose into her life, she suffered for it. It didn't matter that they were best friends as kids, or high school sweethearts, or the most whispered about couple at his brother's wedding. Whenever Zac breezed into her life, she needed to watch out because the only one that ever got hurt was her.

But that's okay, she countered as she set down her brush. She'd learned to deal with it. She'd fantasized about happily ever after with Zac Davidson so many years ago, but came to her senses. The familiar pain tore at her stomach as the consequences of their relationship jolted her, just as it did every time she heard his name. To say it ended poorly was putting it mildly. Never would she be put in that position again. Still, her heart had a mind of its own. Foolishly she'd trusted him the last time he was home, believing he wanted to settle down.

Flicking off the bathroom light, she marched through the house buttoning her shirt and looking for her shoes. She'd handed her heart to Zac twice in her lifetime. Despite the fact he still kissed like a dream, she wasn't about to fall for a third.

Scooping her truck keys out of the ceramic bowl on the table beside the front door, she flicked through the accumulated mail. An envelope from her lawyer caught her eye. If she dug it out, she'd see the emerald green typeset further down the cream colored envelope. Trevor's office was just down from the clinic. She'd stop in after checking the records of the kids coming into camp. Her last session of camp for cancer children started on Monday. Offering a session in September meant more drastic temperature fluctuations, but fall was such a pretty time in Hawk Ridge and the camp registration had filled to capacity. All she could do was put it in God's hands.

The clap of metal on metal rang across the yard as she stepped out of the house. Pulling the door closed behind her, she kept her eyes on the equipment shed across the open parking area. Zac's truck stood parked in the shade of a cluster of Ponderosa pines while he poked at the ancient John Deere settled among a variety of farm implements.

Apprehension grew with her frustration. Couldn't he just leave?

Jen forced her pace to a stroll. As she approached, Zac slapped the door of the tractor and shook his head. He mumbled something she couldn't understand.

Digging her fingers into the tailgate of his pickup, she watched him from across the truck bed. "Zac, what are you doing here?"

"What I was going to do before I heard your death cry. Checking equipment." He stepped out of the shadow of the shed and approached his truck.

No amount of time would ever change the easy swagger that came naturally to Zac Davidson. Jen swallowed as she forced herself not to stare at the wet jeans clinging to strong muscles with each step. His cream colored shirt appeared almost dry with only a few wet blotches outlining his broad shoulders and muscular biceps. A short time ago, those strong, capable arms had held her in welcome, his kiss as familiar as the very breath she took.

She squeezed her eyes shut. *No Lord, not again. I can't do this again.* She drew a breath and opened her eyes as Zac stopped and rested his elbows on the tailgate of his truck.

He nodded toward the slope past the barn. "I'll be haying for the next few weeks."

Alert overrode caution as her nerve endings sparked like blown fuses. "Splint and Max are doing that. And they have plenty of help. They've got most of the hay cut. We're managing fine."

"Jess thinks you need a little help." Zac tipped his ball cap back letting dark hair curl around his temples.

"Jess Eklund? What's Jess got to do with anything?" Her mind stalled at his mention of Arthur Eklund's son. Jess had been nothing but a bully when they were kids. Rumor had it Jess hadn't changed even though he owned one of the most successful steakhouse chains in the state. "Why didn't you tell me that in the kitchen?"

"You were preoccupied." He dragged his hand down his face as if weary of the entire situation. "Jess called me as a friend to oversee the harvest, that's all. Look Jen, that's a lot of acreage to bale and stack. It's going to be tough to finish in a couple of weeks even with all of us working full-time." He waved his hand toward the barn and assortment of out buildings surrounding it. "Why don't you take care of your business, I'll handle mine and we'll all be right where the good Lord wants us."

"Zac Davidson, don't talk down to me." She leapt around the back bumper and planted her feet toe to toe with his, her hand waving toward the barn as he'd done. "*I am* where the good Lord wants me. It's you who's not. Go back to Denver and keep the family business on a financial high - isn't that what you do these days?" Satisfaction flared in her soul as he took a step back from the finger she drilled into his chest. "I can't afford any problems."

"I can work the company numbers anywhere, Bean." He caught her wrist, his grip putting an end to her harping. "What are you talking about? I've been haying my whole life. I know what I'm doing."

"The income off that hay is important to my loan application. I need someone I can depend on. Someone who isn't going to leave when a better offer comes along." She rolled her eyes and blew out a breath. "Max and Splint are working out just fine. They'll get the hay in and make repairs to the house. I've got the camp covered. I've got a lot to prepare or the bank committee won't approve my loan. Don't screw up my system."

He studied her, his deep dark gaze tracing patterns over her face. She could only guess for what he searched. Zac, her childhood friend, rodeoed to his own tune, not caring who he dragged down along the way. His enthusiasm and innocent appeal had been the downfall of many of their adventures. Problem was, Zac never thought ahead to consider if those joining in his schemes knew how to catch themselves before they fell to the rocky ground below. What worked out great for Zac, usually spelled disaster for everyone else.

Three weeks was all she had left before the committee evaluated her proposal to purchase the ranch. She'd been doing fine until Jess Eklund asked to review her business plan incorporating the agricultural acreage. If it were up to Jess, Jen knew he'd try to sabotage her efforts out of spite, if for nothing else. So, on top of her duties as Health Director for the camp, she'd been researching viable options of crop management.

Still, she grudgingly admitted, Zac was right. Even with the three of them directing crews and working full-time, while praying for dry weather and sound equipment, the load pushed the edge of her contractual envelope.

What choice did she have? She had to trust Zac.

"Please, Zac." Jen turned her wrist in his grip until she slid her palm against his, pushing into his solid strength. She didn't know what she was asking of him, all she knew was in a split moment the tides had changed and he held her future in his two strong, more than capable, hands. "I need everything to go right."

The muscles in his cheek worked in concentration just as they had before every rodeo event where he and her brother, Kade, broke the gate after a calf. His skin warmed in her grip. She caught his gaze again and wished she could read his mind rather than just guessing.

His rich brown eyes focused on her as the one side of his mouth tipped up creating a hint of a dimple in his cheek. "You take care of that camp and leave the rest of the place to me."

« CHAPTER TWO »

Tossing her keys into the bowl beside her door, Jen scooped up the day's mail out of habit as she closed the door. *Lord, why is this happening to me?* She dropped her purse in the chair and crossed into the kitchen. Filling a glass with water, she turned and leaned against the edge of the sink. Why? Why was Zac doing this to her? His family had thousands of acres on the Circle D. She couldn't recall Grace or Martin ever mentioning they wanted to buy the Trails' End.

Years ago, Zac couldn't leave Hawk Ridge fast enough. No way would he ever willingly come back.

She stepped over to the table and sank down in the chair. Besides, Arthur Eklund wanted her to have this ranch. He wanted her to provide a safe place for children to heal and mend. She set her glass on the table with a little more force than necessary. She'd had the barn remodeled as the rec center and the old bunk house brought up to handicap building code. Her camp was small now, but she had plans.

A scowl pulled her brows together. Jess Eklund had no right to offer the ranch to his best buddy, Zac Davidson.

Dragging her finger down the side of the glass, she drew through the condensation as a deep breath cleared her mind. No one was going to take her ranch from her. She had everything in place to get the loan. All she had to do was come up with a planting plan. How difficult could that be?

Across the old, scarred oak table mail lay scattered where she'd tossed it. Bills. Advertisements. The same old stuff. Her gaze snagged on the cream-colored envelope so similar to Trevor Hockett's stationary. She pulled it out from between a bill from the local lumber company and an ad for the week's specials at the grocery store. No green foil embossed logo in the corner, just the bold, black lettering of Stone & Stone, A Professional Corporation, Attorneys and Counselors.

Memories of receiving similar correspondence zipped through her brain along with other tidbits of her life better of forgotten.

Her father's proud face when she was awarded her full-ride scholarship...freshman year college...a promising future.

Zac Davidson.

Dreams. Lies. Illusions.

Her mouth went dry even as the edge of the envelope pressed into her moist palm.

She'd received hoards of correspondences from Stone & Stone her freshman year at Denver University. Lisa Morrison, her roommate, had speculated all sorts of scenarios while Jen avoided confiding in her. They were both nursing students, attending on academic scholarships. Both viewed as the cream of the crop of that year's incoming class. Both were expected to set an example. Jen swore not to do anything to dispel that honor and trust.

Until she couldn't hide her pregnancy any longer.

The weekend before finals, Jen melted. She'd gripped the letter from the attorneys in one hand and pounded the dining room table with the other. For six long months she'd successfully avoided the reality of her situation. She'd categorized her pregnancy and slipped her condition into a slot. It helped her not think about it and instead concentrate on classes. On grades. On her future.

One day at a time.

But this letter, this letter was different. Instead of offering suggestions for her to consider when giving a child for adoption, it contained the name of a couple wanting to help her. Wanting her baby. Wanting to relieve her of her burden.

Despite the warm kitchen, an icy shiver raced down her back. A burden. She had viewed God's gift as a burden. Jen squeezed her eyes shut refusing to give into the tears that always surfaced when she thought about her child. Her and Zac's child. A child whom Zac was never to know. She'd handled the situation fine back then, and she'd take her secret to her grave.

Love doesn't pay the bills.

His words from that very afternoon echoed through her mind confirming her decision to surrender their child. They'd been young; they had dreams; they had the rest of their lives before them.

And he never said he'd loved her.

Her eyes misted, but she wiped away the urge to wallow. She took a couple of deep breaths and looked around the kitchen she'd redecorated with a coat of fresh paint and whimsical curtains. It had been a hard decision, one knew she had to make...alone. Every day, the doubt nudged at her conscience; and every day, she refused to wonder if maybe there'd been another way. She closed her eyes as butterflies took flight in her stomach just as they always did when she thought about her daughter, remembering the small miracle of life she'd nurtured for nine months, reliving the time when Zac Davidson had been her whole life. The whispery flutter faded away as it always did, along with the heart gripping pain that used to wrench tears from her. She opened her lids, focusing on the cream envelope with the emerald logo. God had helped her through the most difficult decision of her life and she knew she'd done the right thing. Nothing could ever be worse than giving up her child.

Jen fingered the letter. She hadn't heard from Stone & Stone since the final hearing. Tearing open the envelope with ultimate care, Jen withdrew a single piece of stationary the same cream color as the envelope.

Oh Lord, grant me strength to read this.

The letterhead hadn't changed in twelve years, and neither had the bold signature of Montgomery Stone at the bottom of the page. Her gaze settled on *Dear Ms. O'Reilly...*

She skimmed the rather perfunctory introduction, and then reading word for word the reason for this heart-wrenching intrusion into her life. Air pressed from her lungs as her gaze locked on words. Jen wiped her eyes and focused on the impossible news.

...similar blood type...history of blood disorder...given birth to any other children...

Reading the words over again, and then again, a trail of acid burned from her stomach to her throat.

The paper slid to the floor as she fingered her collarbone. "My baby has cancer."

The walls of the kitchen closed in on her. *Cancer, cancer, cancer.* Faded memories of her mother danced in the shadows of her mind. Her smile, her laugh, her touch. She'd been gone for almost twenty years. Few details remained other than childhood dreams where her mother had held her and promised nothing bad was going to happen.

We'll beat this cancer.

Everything will be fine.

Jen swiped at her eyes and blew her nose into the paper towels she'd grabbed off the counter. She lunged from the table so fast, the chair fell over. She paced around the room, mauling the paper in her grip.

No, nothing had turned out fine. Her mother had died leaving Jen lost, unable to figure out the next step in her life. She swallowed the burning in her throat. She'd wanted to climb in her daddy's lap and hear from him everything would be okay...they were a family...he wasn't going anywhere...they'd always be together. But that wasn't how it worked out. Her dad returned to his practice at the clinic; Kade never came out of his room.

She had no one.

Stopping in front of her living room window, she stared at the playground next to the recently mowed soccer field. A cluster of boys climbed over the log fort built from fallen timbers gathered around the property. The flat-board seats and slings of a sturdy, rustic swing set offered a pair of giggling girls a chance to touch the sky with their toes. A jungle gym of climbing rods, curved slides and colorful canopies stretched across the end of the lot. Minimal equipment for now, and the kids didn't mind the lack of fancy contraptions; they reveled in their ability to navigate the simple therapeutic exercises designed to build their confidence. The whole purpose of this camp was to help the kids strength muscles, build stamina and succeed.

A knot formed in her throat. She never dreamed that one day, her own daughter might be one of these kids.

Grabbing her purse, she ran out the door toward her truck. She'd get more information down at the clinic. History was not going to repeat itself. She planned to fight for whatever medical care available.

Her daughter was not going to die.

Q

"It's so nice having you home." Grace Davidson patted the down comforter on his bed. The dog didn't wait for another invitation and jumped up. "Dinner will be ready in about an hour, and Fletcher, get down."

Zac ruffled the neck of the golden retriever. "It's okay, isn't it boy? This bed is big enough for the both of us." He flopped down making the entire mattress jump.

The old green blanket on his bed spoke of comfort and security. All year 'round, he would kick back on his bed and settle into the comfy softness. No matter how hot the days got, the evenings cooled to a comfortable temp while nights could get downright cold. He'd done some of his best thinking stretched out with his fingers linked behind his head and the smell of softener surrounding him.

His room sat as he'd left it, not a speck of dust to be found. Rodeo buckles lined up on his dresser; football and rodeo team pictures scattered on the wall; the complete set of Hardy Boys mysteries on the bottom shelf of his bookcase. He didn't know whether to draw comfort or alarm from the lack of change. "I'm not very hungry, Mom. Don't make a big deal over me."

"Accept you as a challenge - yes; make a big deal over you - no. Never have; never will. Still, you could use a bit of fussing over. No sense in always being the strong one when you have a perfectly good family ready to rally around you."

"I don't need rallying around."

"Oh, honey," the familiar determination edged with compassion touched her tone, "you do. This is a big change in your life. I never expected you, of all my sons, to move back home. You were always the explorer, the seeker. You were never content here at home, yet, here you are. There's something on your mind whether you realize it or not."

He dug his fingers into the dog's fur and scratched until Fletcher rolled on his back and wiggled. "Why is it so strange that I want to come home? The ranch is here. I can run the financial operations of Davidson Enterprises over the Internet and local bank connections. There's a great highway system just past the ridge and Gunnison has an airport." He turned his palms up, half expecting his mother to fill them with her skewed logic. "Gabe runs the ranching; I run the money. And if Nick ever gets his act together, he was born for PR. If anything, *he's* the one that shouldn't come back to Hawk Ridge -- not that he has a mind to."

"No need for insensitivity, Isaac." Graced swiped her hand at his knee. "We were talking about you, not your brother."

Golden hair and blue eyes came to mind. A laugh that put wind chimes to shame. Jennifer held the key to his dreams nestled on a twenty-four hundred acre spread. "Maybe I'm hungrier than I thought."

"Food's different around here now. Since your father's heart attack," his mother explained as Zac concentrated on the topic of food, not blonds. "I've been trying to find different ways to make chicken taste like beef. It hasn't worked. I don't know what I'd do if Melanie wasn't around. She can convince your father eating sand is good for him."

"Now that, I'd like to see."

"Hush up. Your father hasn't been an easy man to cook for. I tried preparing his favorite dishes like they told me to - substituting this, that and the other - but your dad would have none of it. Melanie comes around with salads and a few fish recipes, and all of a sudden, he's ready to sample the eats of the world."

His sister-in-law had a way with Martin Davidson. Glad to see someone did. His dad had always run the ranch with the attitude of "this is how we've always done it." As the Circle D financial officer, Zac had faced more than one stonewall conversation with his father when suggesting a new investment or commodity avenue. Since Melanie and her son Jason had joined the family, things had changed. For Grace and Martin.

And especially for his brother, Gabe. Shaken up his life; kept him off balance. A completely new experience for the ever dependable Gabriel Davidson.

Tucking one hand behind his head and scratching Fletcher with the other, Zac settled back into the comfortable routine of looking at the world for all it was worth. Being overly responsible had never been his problem. He'd pulled every ounce of adventure out of life. "I'm glad she's making Dad see another side of life."

"Well now, don't go giving her too much credit just because she's getting him to eat egg white omelets and grilled chicken. Your dad is still as stubborn as they come."

Zac raised a brow. "If she can get him to eat egg whites instead of biscuits and gravy, I say there's hope yet."

"Sweetheart, in God's eyes, there's hope for us all." She patted his arm on her way to the door. "Speaking of hope, have you stopped by the Trails' End? Jennifer has done a lot with that place. Does she know you want it?"

"Yeah." His lighthearted mood drained as if flushed from his peace of mind. Their confrontation had scored grooves in his gray matter and touched his buttons. Something Jen had always been good at. "We talked about it."

Grace stopped and slid her hand up the door jamb as her eyes grew wide. "I'll bet that was quite the conversation."

"We established our strengths and weaknesses." The dog writhed beside him as Zac scratched large circles on his belly. "Or something like that."

"That girl's always been strength, Zac." Grace stepped back into the room and faced him. "From the moment her mama died, she bucked up and grabbed life by the horns. She took care of her dad."

Zac sat up and swung his legs over the side of the bed. Fletcher stretched out, reclaiming territory. "And she still thinks it's her job to take care of the world."

"Of course." Grace laughed and shook her head. "That's why you two always got along. She did the thinking; you did the doing. A more Huck and Tom pair I've never seen."

Grace turned and started down the hall toward the kitchen. Zac followed. "Stupid me, I can't think of a single fence that needs whitewashing."

"Whitewashing is just painting old boards to give them new perspective, you know." They stopped in the kitchen. She nodded for him to sit at the counter as she set a bowl of snap peas in front of him. "I wouldn't go glossing over too much of the truth."

He grabbed a hull and snapped the end, pulling the string off with practiced ease. "That ranch is too much for her to handle. Twenty five hundred acres of crops is a lot for anyone to plan, plant and harvest. I'm just trying to make her understand what's involved."

"That's all?" She rummaged through the refrigerator and emerged with a platter of steaks. Setting the plate on the counter across from him, she began trimming off the fat. "This wouldn't have anything to do with the Trails' End once being part of the Circle D, would it?"

"That's just coincidence." He held his tongue, knowing Grace had figured out his motives, but he wasn't ready to acknowledge she'd won. "That spread requires work Jen hasn't even discovered yet. Why else do you think Jess Eklund is all fired up to sell the place?"

"Only the good Lord knows what's on Jess's mind. Just because he can't handle it doesn't mean Jennifer can't. She's a smart girl with a lot of folks believing in her. She's doing a good, productive thing for all those children who need a bit of fun out in the open air."

"I'm not saying that. She's doing a great thing for them. She just doesn't need as much ranch as she's trying to buy." He needed to turn this discussion around before it got out of hand. His mother was a master of getting to the bottom of his dilemmas and weaseling them around to her way of thinking.. "What's wrong with the Carmichael place? It's been for sale for over two years now. I'll bet she could get a great deal if she tried."

Grace never looked up as she scraped the top of the steaks with her paring knife. "Don't forget, Arthur Eklund had faith in her, too. When she made the choice to build this camp idea instead of going to med school, he knew she had the mettle to see it through. You do know Arthur wrote all this out in his will, right? Jen gets first chance at it at the price he set no matter what price Jess wanted to set. Arthur even helped her fix up the barn." She sprinkled seasoning on the last steak and set down her knife, nailing him with her full attention. "You're telling me she's not going to beg, borrow, or negotiate to get the place for that price?"

"I'm not saying she won't, Mom." A dull throb began at the base of his neck, working its way up the back of his head. "I'm just saying I have a back-up contract on the place in case hers falls through."

"Isaac Davidson, you listen to me." Grace plunked her elbow on the counter and sent a couple of jabs of her short paring knife his way. "I raised you to be an honorable man. I know how much you want the Trails' End back in Davidson hands--you've wanted it ever since you heard the whole Jeb Davidson poker game story. But I want you to remember how God does these things." Stopping abruptly, she turned away and shrugged. "I remember a time when you would have done anything for that girl."

So did he. He'd been thinking about it a lot more lately than he should.

And every time he did, the hurt of her abandoning him stung harder. "We were kids. Then we grew up. Happens to most folks."

"You and Jennifer were inseparable. If there was ever a sure thing, it was you and Jen. Still can't believe you parted ways."

Neither could he. He thought they'd have forever. When Jen left for college, she left it all - including him - and never looked back. "We went in different directions, I guess."

"Not so different. You both ended up back home, didn't you?"

"Don't read too much into that."

"Zac, you may have been a headstrong, wild little boy, but you always had a soft heart. You still do, if you'd just trust a little. Have a little faith."

He stopped snapping peas and frowned.

"You say Jennifer doesn't understand the farming end. Well then, help her. Teach her. The good Lord knows what He's doing. Trust Him."

« CHAPTER THREE »

THE ICE CREAM STICK SNAPPED IN HALF.

Glancing down at the splintered ends in each hand, Jen frowned at the distraction. Not a drop of the sweet treat remained on the stick she'd been bending back and forth to calm her nerves. She looked back up at the rooster clock perched on the pine shelf over the kitchen door. A quarter after one. The lab technician said he'd call at noon with the results. Noon. An hour and fifteen minutes ago. What was the hold up?

Jen leaned over the table and shot the half a stick in her hand at the trash can beside the refrigerator. Nailed it. Pressing the other end between her fingers, she set a perfect arc at the can. A satisfying thunk echoed as the stick hit the bottom. Had dread over the test results not been gnawing at her, she'd be whooping up a storm. It had been a week since she'd stopped into the Hawk Ridge Medical Clinic for a cheek swab to see if her DNA matched her daughter's.

A week of chewing her nails, pacing the floor, dusting everything that wasn't nailed down in the house.

If their DNA matched, she'd drop everything and drive to Denver to donate immune building marrow for the transplant. The procedure was simple for the donor. Day surgery to extract the bone marrow and she'd be back in Hawk Ridge before anyone missed her. No one else the wiser; her secret would remain safe.

She followed the line of her laminate counter top to the stove where the leftovers of lunch remained on the cookie sheet. Chocolate chip with walnuts, her favorite comfort food. If the tech didn't call soon, she'd have to bake up another couple dozen. The computer on the other end of the counter beeped indicating a dangerously low battery. Jen turned in her seat. Lot of good her research had done. Carli Seacrest from Canandaigua, New York remained a mystery to Jen, even though she'd given birth to her eleven years ago. She'd scoured the Internet for any information on Carli and her family, but found nothing more in depth than the generic stats Montgomery Stone had given her: a corporate executive father, stay-at-home mother, two other adopted children, water front property on one of the Finger Lakes.

Nothing about Carli. No sports, no hobbies, no pets...nothing. She knew nothing more about this precious little girl to whom she'd given birth than she knew of the sweet children playing in the mountain sunshine just hundreds of feet away from her. They battled cancer. Only the kids at the Trails' End had passed through the fire of treatments and emerged on the other side. Carli still waited at the started block, desperate for her turn to run the race.

Jen banged the heel of her hand on the table causing the clutter of papers in front of her to flutter. The bank was waiting for a business plan from her and all she could do was stare at the clock and count the minutes. She had to snap out of it and get to work. For all she knew, Ray might not call with the results until Monday. Squeezing her eyes shut, she sat up straight in her chair.

Lord, help me focus. The soft whirr of the window fan in the living room clouded her mind like smoke through a keyhole. *Lord, we can do this. Just You and I...just like always.* A gentle calm and quiet settled over her. One step at a time. Don't look for trouble. Take life in stride and move forward. Opening her eyes, she focused on the land map she'd pinned to the wall, her anxieties stuffed away in the back of her mind.

She tilted her head as she stared at all the brightly colored pins scattered across the map.

Drawing a deep breath, Jen followed the twists of an irrigation ditch through the divided crop lands. Nothing was square about this property. All twenty-five hundred acres followed natural ridges and valleys making for a very nice pattern display, but awful for calculating the area. She had a master's degree in nursing--science always came easy to her, not geography. In all, she figured she had eighteen hundred acres of tillable land, fifty flat acres for the camp and the rest in forest and mountainous incline that lent nicely to the trail hikes she'd devised for the campers. The diversity of the property was terrific for what she wanted to do, but at the moment it more than frustrated her. She folded her arms across her chest and stuck her tongue out at the mish-mash of lines in front of her.

"You always did have a creative way of dealing with problems." Zac stood in the kitchen doorway, the screen bouncing into him with a soft thud. "Funny, I seem to remember you nagged at *me* to grow up back in the day."

"What do you want?" Jen continued to stare at her work, afraid to look at Zac. He'd always been able to read her better than she read herself. She didn't want him thinking anything was wrong. If he so much as offered her the smallest comfort, she feared her nerves would shred.

"I came to apologize."

Her ears perked even as the rest of her body froze in place.

"I should have told you about the contract. I asked Trevor to draw it up because he's most familiar with the details. I asked him not to tell you."

At his confession, an iron knot tightened in her stomach. She had her own secrets, but she wasn't about the return the confession. Ever since discovering Zac's opinion on love and money, her resolve to keep her secret only strengthened. If all worked out, she'd be a match, take care of her daughter's health and no one would be the wiser.

She turned her head until she caught a glimpse of Zac leaning against the door jamb, his palm flattened on the counter top. In a button down shirt with his sleeves rolled to the elbow, his darkly tanned arms proved he was more an outdoors man than one to sit behind a desk. "Trevor," --her voice cracked-- "told me."

He nodded, his thick, dark hair brushing the collar of his shirt making him look like a kid out of school rather than the CFO of a corporation. "I asked him not to say anything unless you asked. I put him in just as uncomfortable a position as I have you. I'm sorry."

What was she supposed to say to his naked confession? Throw a fit? Throw him out? He'd pulled the rug out from under her righteous indignation. Rat. She turned back toward her work. "It's a back-up contract. Doesn't mean you're getting the ranch, but it probably makes Jess feel better about a deal."

"Exactly. I'm glad you understand." He ventured closer and waved his finger at the wall. "That wall is going to need some serious spackle once you finish your crop plan.."

"I'm remodeling bit by bit anyway." She didn't have the energy to spar with him. Thoughts of her daughter blended with the reality of Zac. So foreign, yet so familiar. Both beyond her grasp. She drew a breath and waved him over. "C'mon closer, I promise I won't bite."

His dark eyes lit with his smile as he hooked the chair beside her. "A nibble here or there wouldn't hurt."

The familiar ribbing loosened her up. In no time at all, he'd distracted her enough for the muscles in her shoulders to relax and the tension to drain from her neck. She shifted her hips and moved over to give him a better view of her work. "Goon."

Their shoulders bumped as he studied the map, the contour of his solid muscles obvious through the fabric of his shirt. "Where did you get this? The layout is old." He leaned toward the wall and traced lines that traveled all over the map. "The overall boundary is the same, but a couple of these fields have split due to diverted irrigation patterns."

All she heard was *layout* and *fields* as Dial soap and Old Spice aftershave played with her senses and mingled with the familiar scent of his warm skin. Some things never changed. Frustration stirred. The past was the past, right? Her back molars ground as she fought to keep her emotions locked up.

Think clearly, girl. Think ahead.

Even as the warning shouted through her head, Jen drew another wiff of Zac's famous brand of strength and attraction. Tough thinking about timothy hay and flood irrigation with his strong forearm right next to her cheek. When she turned her head, her hair brushed his sleeve and she practically jumped out of her seat.

He glanced at her. "You okay?"

Figures and graphs lay scattered in front of her. He traced a blunt finger down the weathered paper on the table. Growth charts and seeding patterns took back seat to the strong, tanned hands marred with scars from a lifetime spent team roping with her brother. The two of them had been quite the pair, becoming fast friends when the O'Reilly children had been temporarily adopted into the Davidson family. Before their mother had died, Kade barely knew which end of the horse to point toward the steer.

Jen cleared her throat. "Have you seen my brother lately?"

His fingertip stopped at the bottom of the column. "Yeah, I just saw him last month. What made you ask?"

Her gaze swiped over his thumb, the tip still bent at an unnatural angle from a roping incident so many years ago. The guys were always careful, but trouble found them anyway. Zac and Kade had endured their share of injuries. "Just wondering. I haven't seen him since Easter."

Zac rested his elbow on the back of her chair, his hand grazing her neck as he studied her. Her pulse sprinted even as she angled away from him. The sight, sound and smell of Zac Davidson messed with her head.

"He stopped by the office in Denver on his way to Steamboat Springs. Mitch Cauldwell has him hauling bulls up and down the Front Range from New Mexico to Montana for all the rodeos running." A tiny frown formed between his well-shaped brows. "I thought he said he was stopping home before going north."

"If he did, I didn't see him." Her gaze avoided his questioning brown eyes. "Dad didn't say anything either."

"Does your dad still want him to go back to school?"

The image of her irate dad flashed across her mind. "I think I have enough education for the both of us, but he thinks Kade should do more than drive stock for a cattle company. He'd be happy if Kade thought about getting a more challenging job."

"Cauldwell Cattle Company is big. Maybe Kade's holding out for a promotion. I know my brother Nick thinks the world of Mitch Cauldwell. . .and Nick doesn't think well of most people."

"Nick's trying to win rodeos on Cauldwell bulls. He better chum up to the right people. If I remember correctly, Nick didn't think too much of Jess Eklund's riding abilities."

"Jess didn't have any bull riding ability. I believe my brother stated that blunt enough after one particularly ugly ride. Jess could care less about Nick's opinion and Nick never could suffer fools. He told me to keep Jess in my prayers until the good Lord succeeded in pounding some sense into the kid." Zac stretched his arms over his head, his shirt pulling tight across his chest. "Jess wasn't much better at bronc riding, so I kept praying for him."

Jen ignored the image of masculine perfection in front of her and turned her attention to the map tacked to the wall. "How can you still be friends with Jess Eklund?"

A slow laugh lifted his chest. "You still mad at him after all these years?"

"I'm not mad," she defended. "I never was."

"Right." Zac cocked his head to the side. "You and Jess got along like oil and water all through school. You knew he was just a lot of hot air. You should have ignored him. At least forgiven and forgotten, by now."

"He's still making my life miserable. If it wasn't for him, the bank never would have asked for this stupid business plan."

"Of course they would've." He leaned closer until she could see the hint of evening whiskers on his face. She stared at the pattern of black and gray lines etched within his brown eyes. Brown eyes that gleamed, appearing just as taken with staring at her.

"The bank needs to know you're up to the job," he coaxed, his voice low and rough. "Jess is protecting his family assets."

Jen cleared her throat, a lump of unwelcome longing choking her voice. "He's selling off the family assets. His dad wanted the ranch to go to kids who needed it most; Jess wants the money."

"Jess and his dad never saw eye to eye but that doesn't make him a bad guy."

She struggled to subdue her irritation. "Don't defend him to me, Zac. Don't you remember all the times you stuck up for me and told him to leave me alone? He was nothing but a big bully then, and he's not any better now."

Zac drew closer. A hint of mint on his breath and the scent of pure male mingled with soap tangled about her. "He's my friend. You were my girl. You think I had an easy time of it back then?"

Her lips moved, but words escaped her. Dark waves brushed across his forehead, the tips of his hair lightened from the sun. Color brushed across his cheeks from the strong, mountain sun making the light in his dark eyes bright. Would she ever get be able to get Zac Davidson out of her system? A retort formed on her lips just as her cell phone rang. Snapped out of an all too familiar spell, she shook her head. No daydreams; no happily ever afters. Needing distance, Jen got up and walked out onto the porch.

"O'Reilly speaking."

"Jennifer O'Reilly? This is Marcia from Nuberg Labs." The woman exuded calm over the the miles. "We have your results."

@

Jennifer O'Reilly was still one hot girl.

Zac watched her walk out the kitchen door and onto the back porch, her cell phone clamped tightly to her ear. He couldn't help but smile. She used to get hopping mad at him when they were kids. He'd give her room and let her cool off, and before long, they'd be playing, or riding, or kissing...depending on their ages at the time.

Tracing the wood grain of the table top with his finger, he shook his head. He'd never known what to expect from Jen, and at the same time, he knew exactly what to expect. She needed her ducks in a row, the details worked out before she joined any of his adventures. She had to know what she was getting into, and if he didn't have the answers, she'd pester him until he found them for her. Jess Eklund, his best friend? Jen obviously never had a clue. No matter what she thought about Jess Eklund or even her brother, Jen had always been his best friend.

And girlfriend.

The convergence point of all things sensible and solid.

Until she dumped him.

He never even knew why she disappeared from his life. She'd been sad they were going to different schools, even though he'd assured her nothing would change. They saw each other as they could, but after a couple of months, she stopped calling and accepting his phone calls. He even stopped by her apartment in Denver a couple of times only to be turned away by her roommate who adamantly assured him Jen wasn't home and she had no idea when she'd be back.

Right. He recognized a brush off when he got one.

A couple of minutes had passed and he realized he hadn't heard her voice. Out on the porch, Jen stood braced against the newel post at the edge of the steps. A breeze teased at the ends of her blonde hair making him want to twist the strands between his fingers just like he used to do. Funny, he never thought he'd say it, but he could get used to Jennifer O'Reilly back in his life. Their split was so far in the past, he barely remembered if he'd missed her at all at the time. His heart began to pound as caution signals pumped up to his brain.

Liar.

The hole in his heart had never mended, but Zac was a firm believer in what happened in the past, stayed in the past. They were both older and wiser now. Why not? Especially since he planned to offer her a deal she couldn't refuse. And since she'd not be able to refuse him, their close proximity alone would work in his favor for maybe picking up where they'd left off all those years ago.

For now, he had to quit grinning. After she conceded to his wisdom, *then* he could grin all he wanted.

Jen continued to slump beside the post. Maybe she enjoyed the breeze after sitting in the stuffy kitchen all morning.

Standing, he headed out to the porch. She didn't move a muscle as the door slammed behind him. "Hey, we were working remember?"

She didn't look up. She leaned her elbow on the rail, her phone clasped in her palm. "I need a minute, okay?"

Warning alarms rang through his head. When Jen pulled away, it usually meant bad news. He didn't want to push it, or push her. He hadn't been back in her life long enough to even assume she wanted to share anything with him. Still, seeing her in obvious distress didn't set well with him. "Can I help?"

She didn't answer. If anything, her shoulders slumped a bit more.

"I'm sorry for whatever bad news you just got, but maybe my news can raise your spirits a bit. I studied the layout of the Trails' End. You want the house, barn and the outbuildings for your camp. I want the fields and crops. We can work through this and figure out how to make both our dreams come true. Especially for the camp."

She tilted her chin and looked up at him, her eyes dull and mouth straight. It wasn't much, but at least he got her attention. He ran with that little crumb of encouragement. "How does this sound -- I'll buy the ranch and draw up a lease giving you and the camp perpetual access to the agreed upon acreage. I'll even work in improvements over the course of your lease as the camp grows."

Jen straightened from the railing, her back propped against the support post. Her gaze darted around everywhere but meeting his. Zac didn't know if this was a good move, but at least he'd gotten a reaction. When she opened her mouth to speak, he rushed in and cut her off.

"Don't make a decision right now. I know it sounds sketchy at best, but believe me, we can make this happen. You're still trying to find funding and from the looks of the crop rotations you're working on, there is a lot of gray area in your knowledge to secure any loans. I can help you, if you just let me."

Her fingers curled around the phone as the heel of her boot stomped on the porch boards. She finally met his gaze, her blue eyes bright with moisture. "Zac--"

"It will work, Jen." He interrupted again, expectant, yet afraid of her response. "We were a great team once. Together we can build this place, make it the best working ranch camp it can be. It'll be fun."

Moistening her lips, her mouth returned to same grim line. She held up the hand and waved her phone at him. "No preparation in the world will help me get these words right, so I'm not even going to try." Tears brimmed, but none spilled over. "You've got a daughter, Zac, and she's going to die unless we can help her."

A daughter? No way he'd heard that right. Her chin trembled making the hairs on his forearms rise. Jen never cried, not even when she had good reason. "What?"

Her fingers curled tightly around her phone as her fist pumped up and down. "You...you and I...we had a daughter," she said softly. "A long time ago. She's sick now. She needs a bone marrow transplant."

Daughter? Cancer? Acid spiked the middle of his gut as memories busted out of the depths of his heart. The dreams - and the love - they'd shared. Whispered commitments to each other that hadn't amounted to more than passion for the moment.

Jen squared him with a steady gaze despite the moisture making her blue eyes sharp and brilliant. Apprehension grew and he tamped it down into oblivion, giving it a spin out of pure self-preservation. "One of your camp kids needs help? How can I help?"

The slow shake of her head made it impossible to misconstrue the truth. Bitterness rose in his throat. "How? When?"

Pushing away from the post, she squared her stance and swiped away the tears rolling down her cheeks. Her capable, nurse persona slipped into place. "A long time ago." She crossed her arms, her fingers locked into her elbows giving the appearance of an immovable force. "I gave her up for adoption. To a very good family."

"Our baby?" Giving voice to his fears only shocked him more.

Silence.

His mind spawned dozens of scenarios to justify the information given him. Some viable; some ridiculous. Some simply outrageous.

"Is this some sick way of getting back at me?" Her lack of response made his anger burn hotter. "Your life was always lined up. Every piece in place. Have I messed up your plans? Broken a link in your tidy chain?" Even as the cruel words poured out of his mouth, he knew the truth and it did not set him free.

The color drained from her face. "No."

He barely heard her as the enormity of the situation crashed around him. Talons of betrayal ripped through his heart. She'd had a child...their child...a child he'd never known about. The realization made him sway as he reached up and pinched the bridge of his nose. And their child had cancer.

⟪

Her life had never lined up. Zac had been the only constant in her life. After her mother had died, Jen had counted on him to be there for her...and then he wasn't. A whole new world had opened up to him and he'd embraced it with gusto. "No."

"No, what? You hate me, or I messed up your plans?"

"Neither." Thoughts and feelings long subdued shot to the surface and she didn't know how to stop them. She motioned to the wicker furniture arranged beneath the window. "Zac, can we sit down?"

"I'd rather stand as my world explodes around me."

Jen hiked a hip onto the porch railing and prayed for the right words to explain, to make him understand. "*We* messed up our plans. *We* were invincible the summer before college, remember? Plans, dreams, freedom all lay before us - before both of us, Zac. You were leaving for Colorado State and I was packed for DU." She pushed away from the railing and began to pace. "Had a great apartment lined up just off campus with a roommate chosen for me like something out of an Internet dating site."

She took a breath, undaunted by the uncompromising jut of his chin. "*That's* having your life all lined up. Classes, books, friends all waiting for you to walk in and begin a new life. The only thing missing in the whole picture was familiarity and heart." She stopped back at the newel post by the steps and looked out over the hillside covered in pine trees backed up to her house. Vast and serene, a slice of mountainside she could only appreciate now that the past was behind her. The whole ranch became a fortress for her when she finally realized God's plan for her life, that she'd never been alone. She squinted along the ridge line, following a trail of cone studded pines until she returned back down to the porch and met Zac's wary brown eyes. She dropped her gaze.

"Yeah, I was excited to begin my nursing degree, but nothing was *lined up* in my life."

"Are you telling me you were homesick? After all the plans we'd made? You wanted back home?"

"That was the last thing I wanted." Recognizing the disgusted tone, she dug her fingertips into the railing. "You found your new life." The cruel memory of walking into the lobby of his dorm wisped through her brain. She shook it away before the details played out. "I got what I wanted, and so did you."

"What did I get?"

A creak of the porch board warned her he'd stepped closer. He stood beside her now, a lifetime too late for everything she'd wanted to say to him. And everything she wanted him to say to her.

"Neither one of us was ready to raise a child, Zac." A breeze blew her hair across her cheek. "I made a decision I thought was best."

"You were pregnant and handled it alone?" He grabbed his ball cap and pulled it off before driving his fingers through his hair. "I don't buy it. Maybe the kid wasn't mine."

His words stabbed deep in her heart. She lifted her head and met his defiant glare. "I forgive you for saying that."

He blew a breath as he fit the cap back in place. "So why didn't you tell me?"

"I tried to once, but couldn't go through with it. I wasn't going to ruin the life you'd dreamed about for so long." Her stomach turned at the memory of their moonlight talks back in high school filled with the big what-ifs of life. They'd shared their innocent dreams, their eager anticipation of finding out what the world held for them. The promises they'd made to one another, promises carrying as much weight as the breath they'd been delivered on in the heat of the moment. "You couldn't wait to get out of Hawk Ridge. I didn't want to drag you back. I didn't want you to resent me."

Zac stood silently, digesting the secret she'd held alone for so many years. The Zac of years ago would have thrown a tantrum and denied the claim. Jen didn't know what to expect out of the Zac that stood before her today. "I didn't want you to resent us."

"So you just took the decision out of my hands because you didn't think I could handle it?" his tone strung so tight it cracked. "Wasn't that just martyr-ly of you."

"I didn't know what to think, Zac," she snapped and began to pace across the porch. "I didn't know what to do. I was eighteen years old. I was scared. I had no one to turn to. I prayed and prayed for an answer and then prayed some more...and still, I wasn't sure." Her emotions collided as memories boiled to the surface. "Being a martyr had nothing to do with it. I didn't want to disappoint you, I didn't want to disappoint my dad." She stopped back at the railing and looked out along the pine-covered slope. "But that's exactly what I was -- a big, fat disappointment."

She fought the tears, yet they spilled down her cheeks anyway. "I couldn't go home. I couldn't run to you. All I could do was ask God for direction, and I didn't get a whole lot of that either." Brushing at her cheek, she confronted the last demon on her list. "If your parents found out, they would've made you do the right thing. I couldn't let that happen."

He turned from her and planted his hands on the railing, dragging in a deep breath. "You more than anyone--" he stopped, the veins in his neck protruding along side muscle and tendons. "I thought you believed in me. I thought you knew me."

Jen leaned closer, trying to catch his soft words. Her own thoughts jumbled together...a couple of months out of Hawk Ridge, he'd found the life he'd dreamed of...and it hadn't included her. "I knew you; I knew me. I knew we weren't old enough to take responsibility for a new life. I did the best I could."

"You decided for the both of us."

"You'd moved on."

He straightened, his movements stiff and pained. Folding his arms across his chest, his biceps strained within the confines of his sleeves. "How do you know what I felt?"

"I had a pretty good idea." Jen didn't want to dig any deeper into the memories she'd kept closed away for so long. She certainly didn't want to open the door and let them spring out all over Zac. She wasn't ready for that yet.

"You always thought you knew it all," he said with a rawness that tore between them. "You never had a clue."

« CHAPTER FOUR »

THE LAST FEW BITES of his sister-in-law's savory chicken potpie stuck in his throat like paste on a pinata.

"Good to have you home, Zac." Melanie passed a bowl of seasoned zucchini to him as the family sat around his parents' kitchen table. "After two years of being a part of this family, I'm looking forward to getting to know at least one of Gabe's brothers."

"You got the prize out of this litter, Mel. You might think you want to get to know them, but really, you don't." Gabe grinned with pride.

Zac grabbed his glass of water and took a long drink. Gabe's wife, Melanie, knew how to make meals tasty and heart healthy. Even six months pregnant with twins, she insisted on cooking for the entire family whenever Gabe gave the go ahead. For a man who swore he'd never get married, Gabe hit the marital jackpot when Melanie and her son had literally crashed into his life.

That crash didn't compare to the explosion Jen had detonated only hours earlier. He set the glass down and picked up his fork, stirring a piece of crust with the tines. He prided himself on knowing what he wanted in life and going after it. How did he deal with this foul ball? The familiar dinnertime banter surrounding him should have bolstered his mood, but instead, left him feeling like a complete and total alien.

He'd fathered a child. Did he tell his family? What happened next? He herded a small group of peas with his fork to the center of his plate.

"Don't you listen to him, Melanie." Grace Davidson buttered her dinner roll in complete oblivion to her son's dilemma. "Nick and Zac are fine men. They've been about their business and visit when they can."

Grace nudged him with his elbow when he didn't respond. With a frown, Zac stabbed a pea, sending it spinning across his plate. "I get home when I can. I'm here; Nick's not. Pick on him."

"Oh, dear, we're not picking on anyone." Grace shooed Gabe's anticipated retort away. "It's always nice to be remembered by your children. When they have the time."

"Grace, the boy is home, quit nattering at him." Martin swallowed and pointed at her with his fork. "Pass the potatoes."

"I'm not nattering at him. I simply--"

"Dad, it's alright." Zac nodded at Martin and grabbed his plate. He had no business ruining the conversation at the table with his mood and he certainly didn't want his mother wheedling it out of him. "I've been away awhile, but now I'm home. Excuse me, I need some air." Placing his dishes in the sink, he grinned at Melanie as he slapped Gabe on the back. "I can see why my brother has picked up a few pounds. Great meal. Thanks."

"Hey," Gabe protested. "It's all muscle."

"That's what you've been telling me for years, bro." Zac pulled open the door and gave his brother the once over. "Looks good on you."

A hint of fall nip greeted him as he stepped out onto the porch that ran the distance of the house. The slight wind carried the scent of pine and timber, wrapping him in the peace of home. No matter how far he traveled or how long he stayed away, the homestead kept a power draw on him. A draw he fought no more.

He stepped over to a pair of wooden rocking chairs. The chairs had been there ever since he could remember. A small table now sat between them and a three cushion glider added additional seating. He sank down into the floral print of the chair closest to the railing and and propped his booted feet up on the handrail, staring across the drive at the corrals and old, black barn. Little had changed, yet everything had changed. What had Jen been thinking? If he'd given her a car and she'd chosen to sell it because they'd broken up, he wouldn't have thought twice about it. But a child? They created a child together and she gave it away?

My child. She gave away my child.

Anger, confusion, despair all clamored for attention in his brain. All rational thought escaped him and he bowed to the whim of emotions. A mixed-up, turned-around, unfathomable churn of emotions.

"Zac?"

He jumped at the soft voice. Not two feet away, Melanie stood beside him, her brows drawn together as she studied him.

How could a woman so obviously uncomfortably large move so quietly?

"Zac, are you awake? Is it okay if I join you? Gabe won't let me do the dishes, so I thought I'd better just get out of the way."

"Sure. Have a seat." His feet hit the porch with a thud as he shifted in his chair and faced her. Talking was the last thing he wanted to do. "Too much action in the kitchen?"

She sank onto the glider, stretching her legs across the cushions. "Way too much. Grace moves around that table like war planes at two o'clock. I could've stayed in the corner and listened to her tell Gabe he was washing dishes all wrong, or I could come out and cool off in the early fall evening air. I think I chose wisely."

"For your sanity, I think you did, too." Zac grinned in the deepening dusk. He really liked Melanie. She had a way of cutting to the heart of the matter without caring if the other person wanted to hear her opinion or not. You knew where you stood with her.

Yep. He liked her a lot. "What does Jason think about being a big brother soon?"

"He's a coward about it, just like Gabe. The thought of gaining two sisters at once is a bit intimidating." Melanie laughed. "Before I married Gabe, Jason didn't really know what family life was like. He had no idea having a dad and grandparents could be so much fun. And now, he's about to have siblings. "

Her smile faded as she looked across the yard toward the mountain peaks. "Jason never knew his father. He'd abandoned us when I got pregnant. We weren't married - hadn't even discussed the option. My parents and I didn't see eye to eye on how I should handle the situation. I kept my final decision from them for years. Jason didn't meet my parents until a couple of years ago."

The conversation hit close to home. Same circumstances; different ending. "Why did you do it then? Keep the baby, I mean?"

At her silence, Zac realized he'd stepped over some serious privacy bounds. "Sorry, Melanie, I didn't mean to pry. Forget I asked. *Please* forget I asked."

"It's okay, Zac. Really." She shifted on the settee and stuffed a throw pillow behind her. "It wasn't an easy decision to make. I knew I wasn't going to terminate the pregnancy like Paul wanted me to do. My parents decided adoption was the only course I could consider. No one asked me what I wanted to do. Good thing too, because I didn't have a clue. So, I prayed."

The sounds of the night closed in around them and the wind blew just hard enough to keep the mosquitoes away. Zac leaned toward her, not wanting to miss a word. Never before had he thought about unplanned pregnancies or what women did about them. Now all of a sudden, the information and circumstances were coming at him from every angle. Voices sounded from the kitchen along with cabinet doors closing and footsteps crossing back and forth. The dishes were almost done. *Please, Lord, I want to hear the end of the story.*

"I didn't think God heard my prayer for the longest time. I didn't gain any great wisdom or see a path to follow. I prayed throughout my pregnancy for direction and all I got was help, support and assistance from everyone I knew. I didn't recognize it at the time, but God had answered my prayers all along. I went into labor and delivery thinking I'd talk to someone at the hospital about giving up my baby." Her voice trailed as she smiled at him, a smiling full of joy and compassion. Zac stared, too engrossed to realize how close he'd leaned toward her until she sat forward practically nose to nose with him.

"When they placed him in my arms, I knew I was never going to let him go."

Her whispered words seemed to draw him into her secret circle of understanding. She'd shared her deepest maternal instincts with him and they touched his very soul.

"If I had made arrangements for an agency to take him away before I ever got to hold him, my life would be completely different right now. I wouldn't have a terrific son, or a wonderful husband, or about to be blessed with the gift of twins." She rubbed her palm over her enormous belly and leaned back against the pillow again. "I might have had an easier life, but then, I would have missed out on this one."

An easier life. The light of understanding clicked on in Zac's brain. Jen had always like things stacked neatly, all her options in a row. When they were kids, she'd hated anyone messing up her plans. A child was definitely a messy thing. He glanced at Melanie as she rocked gently on the glider, her hand rubbing her enormous belly. Zac frowned and leaned back into his chair, focusing across the corral at the shadows of the mountain peaks. But neat and tidy were nothing compared to rigors of life. And, if the pregnancy had inconvenienced her, why did she go full term?

That thought almost caused him to roll off his chair. Jen would never have considered abortion. No matter how the circumstances were spun, he'd never think of Jen as being heartless, if anything, she cared too much.

Still, the thought rolled around in his brain. She'd practiced for years as a pediatric oncology nurse. She'd nurtured and cared for children on the brink of death. So, she could care for children as long as they didn't follow her home at night? That didn't make sense. Frankly, nothing made sense about anything anymore.

He began to rock back and forth, the porch boards creaking in an even rhythm as a knot tightened in his gut. How would he have felt if the responsibility of raising the child had fallen on him? He couldn't see it, but that didn't mean he wouldn't have risen to the challenge. Resting his feet back on the railing, he crossed his hands over his stomach and tapped his thumb on his belt buckle.

Something told him there was more to the story, but the obvious spoke louder. The hurt of Jen dumping him in college still stung, even though he'd managed to stuff that hit away and rarely gave the scar of heartache a passing glance anymore. Up in the sky the stars dotted the heavens, the picturesque scene lost on Zac as his mind struggled to grasp some sort of understanding of the situation.

She'd given up their child. What had he done to deserve that?

(Q

"Enjoy the day the Lord has made!"

Cheers rose in the recreation building as Patrick, the head camp counselor gave the closing to the devotion. The kids broke rank and ran out the door, Jen not even urging caution. She picked up a couple of stray napkins and threaded through the maze of chairs. God had granted the campers gorgeous days for this late in the summer. She hoped and prayed the mild weather held for another couple weeks.

"Quite a crew they've been through this session." Patrick grabbed a couple chairs and clapped them into stacks. "You've had a great season running the camp all by yourself, Jennifer."

She couldn't help but agree the first three sessions had gone well, and with this one wrapping up, her summer appeared emergency-free. "You just keep covering all those kids in prayer and winding them up for the day and we'll have a terrific time. What are the plans?"

"Cheryl and Janet had to leave early. Last year of college for them both. Wanted to get back to Denver and get settled in before classes started."

"Can't blame them. I was antsy to finish, too." She pushed the stack of chairs up against the wall. "Are we short-handed for the last group coming up?"

"Not really. We've had forty-five campers the other sessions. This time we only have thirty-five. And with news spreading about this great program, I've got volunteers coming out of the woodwork. I think we'll manage."

"I can't believe families want to come up in September. The nights will be cold."

"It's our prettiest time of the year, though." Patrick indicated the group playing just outside the barn door. "The kids are sturdy, we'll be okay."

"I'm ready for winter break." Jen wiped her brow of mock sweat. "I'm worn out."

"You just need a spark in your life." He nudged her on the shoulder as his infectious laugh filled the empty recreation hall.

Five years older and a hundred times more energetic, Patrick Marsh held more optimism in his little finger than Jennifer could muster out of her entire five-foot-ten-inch frame. Not fair in the least. Where all Jen wanted was to drag home at the end of the day, he came alive and entertained at the campfire and then watched movies with the kids until lights out.

Every summer camp needed a Patrick Marsh. She thanked God every night he'd been assigned to the Summit Camp at Trails' End by the Mercy Life faculty. Between directing the health program at the camp, working with sponsors and developing a business plan, she barely had enough energy to glow much less to ignite sparks.

"Sparks lead to fire." She pointed out. "Fires burn forests and forest fires cause camp evacuations. How about we think more along the lines of water sports?"

"Kill joy." A hint of curiosity colored his voice as he glanced out the window toward the playground. "So, what's the story with the cowboy?

Heat raced through her so fast, Jen thought she'd ignite despite her prior dousing of sparks. "The owner of the property brought him in to oversee the haying." She forced a smile. "Glad Zac's here to do it. Didn't know how I'd keep track of all the physical asset responsibility of the property."

"Zac, is it now?" Patrick eyed her. "Mighty chummy for a cowboy new to the place."

Jennifer turned from his all-knowing stare. Patrick's penchant for curiosity had caught her off guard many times. "New to the Trails' End, but not to Hawk Ridge. I've known him forever. No big deal."

"Maybe he can give you some business plan pointers. If he's up here to look after the harvest, he probably knows ways to make it profitable."

The familiar stomp of boots across the pine grain laminate floor made Jen perk up. Hadn't Zac said he needed to go to town? She turned just as he stopped beside her, looking all solid and handsome, and smelling undeniably wonderful. The hairs on the back of her neck rose. Last time they'd talked, he'd peeled out of her parking lot, dirt and gravel spewing from all four tires.

She glance up quickly and tensed at his easy smile. She didn't buy it. "Zac--"

"This lodge is great." He cut her off. "No wonder Jess is worried about the harvest coming in to make a loan payment. I've never seen the whole looking so good." Zac stuck out his hand. "Zac Davidson. Hired hand."

Patrick accepted the offer with a firm shake. "Patrick Marsh, camp counselor. Jennifer mentioned Splint and Max were about to get some direction in their duties."

Zac gave a low chuckle that warmed Jen right in the pit of her belly, reminding her of years gone by. Before thoughts of love had entered the picture.

Before *complicated* became her byword. Before she had to share her secret.

She swallowed to clear her throat. "The guys know what they're doing."

"'Course they do," Zac agreed easily. "They just need another pair of hands to get it done. They've already completed most of the cutting but we've got a lot of acres to cover and I doubt Jen here has the time to bale and stack hay."

"Sums it up pretty much even though this camping session is a little smaller than the others. We've always got to keep an eye out for the kids and their safety." Patrick nodded toward the playground. "Speaking of which, I've got a soccer game to organize before there's mutiny. Tonight's movie night, Zac. Why don't you stop by?"

"Chances are I'll be cutting until late. Thanks for the invite, though."

Patrick waved as he trotted off toward the game.

"Can I have a word with you? In private?"

The bile in her stomach rose to her throat. "I really should be helping Patrick."

"This will only take a minute."

She nodded, wrapping her arms across her midsection. Turning the corner, she led him to a darkened alcove Patrick used as his office. Unless they wanted to go to the clinic or back to the ranch house, this was as private as they were going to get. Probably a good idea to keep a potentially volatile conversation within sight of witnesses.

"I can't begin to understand this entire situation so I'm not going to pretend. It's going to take me a long time to figure things out - time this little girl probably doesn't have." He began to pace within the confines of the minuscule space, clasping his hands and rubbing his thumb into his palm. "I've played every scenario possible through my mind and I always end up at the same place - if I wasn't a blood relative, it would be pretty difficult for me to be a match. And why would you drag me into this if I wasn't a viable possibility?"

He stopped in front of her. Even by the dim light filtering around the cork partition from the rec area, Jen noticed the dark circles under his eyes. She wanted to sweep all this heartache and grief away. But it was a bit late for wishful thinking.

"Is this girl-"

"Carli. Her name is Carli."

"Is Carli really my child?"

Tears stung her eyes. "Yes."

She couldn't tell if resignation or burden caused his shoulders to slump. His jaw worked, bunching the muscles in an erratic rhythm.

Jennifer couldn't take it anymore. "Let me show you something."

Clicking on the button of Patrick's computer monitor, Jen logged into the system and typed in the Internet address she'd never be able to erase from her mind. Giving the system a moment to locate the site, she angled the monitor toward Zac.

"Zac, meet your daughter."

℗

A fission of dread raced up his spine.

Zac stopped pacing and stood beside the desk piled high with folders and books, and a desktop computer vintage last decade if he recognized his PC models. Jen's fingers raced over the keyboard, her series of taps and spaces tipped him off she'd done this a time or two. Her blue gaze flitted over the screen a second before she turned the monitor for him to see.

A picture of a little girl wearing a cowboy hat filled the sidebar beneath a banner proclaiming a social site for a hospital Minnesota. Wisps of hair curled beneath the brim of the white hat as big dark eyes crossed for the camera atop a smile that brightened the darkened corner where he stood. The column next to the photo proclaimed, *Carli Seacrest - This is my story!*, in bold, purple lettering.

"It was basic research." Jen said, her voice wavering as she stood from the chair. "The oncology kids we treated in Denver all had support pages for family and friends to cheer them on. I knew Carli would have one, I just needed to find it."

She motioned for him to have a seat. Zac eased into the armless chair, never taking his eyes off the screen. The little girl in the picture had his brown eyes, but the shape of her face was all Jennifer, up to and including the natural, silly facial gestures. The white hat stood in stark relief to her dark hair - poor thing, she even had the same unpredictable wave to her hair as him.

Hi, I'm Carli. I'm 11 years old and I love riding horses.

The muscles in Zac's throat constricted as he read her introduction. She liked to dance and loved every kind of animal. Her daddy was a lawyer and her mom stayed home with her and her two brothers.

"There are more pictures of her and the family if you go here." Jen pointed at the top bar.

Without stopping to think, he clicked on the tab and a series of snapshots filled the screen. Carli looked tall and thin, dwarfed by who he assumed were her brothers, as they stood in front of a rowboat at a lake. Zac scanned the photos and clicked on more screens, more pictures of a happy family doing family things except for the shots taken at the hospital. He swallowed as he followed the progression of the disease that had robbed this family of their contentment. In some photos, Carli had long, dark wavy hair that she wore in all manner of messy styles - just like Jen used to wear her hair. In the latest photos, Carli sported a ball cap, the brim falling low across her brows. Pain etched its mark at the corners of her eyes and mouth, but her dimpled cheek spoke volumes for the hope that lived in her heart.

"You can even leave a note for her in the guest book."

Her words had barely left her lips before Zac pushed the button to darken the screen and stood from the chair. He didn't know what he was expecting but recognizing the family resemblance in this stranger knocked him off kilter. Not only a family resemblance to him, but to him and Jennifer O'Reilly combined. An icy lump settled in his stomach. There was no doubt in his mind that Carli was his daughter, but his heart still had some accepting to do. And it wasn't all revolving around the role of *this* girl in his life.

There wasn't much time to think about it. Zac began pacing again, his fingers jammed into the pockets of his jeans.

"I'll go in for the swab. If I'm a match, I'll donate my bone marrow to help the gir-" He shook his head, the notion of having a daughter still too new to him. "To help Carli. As far as the medical end goes, that's as far as I've gotten."

"I appreciate --" she began to thank him until he abruptly stopped and faced her. Her round, blue eyes shown bright in the limited light. If he didn't talk fast, Jen would start to cry and then all his resolve would wash away like the tears rolling down her cheeks. He had to cut bait and run, and leave no doubt in anyone's mind over where he stood on her deceit.

"As far as you and I go..." his voice went flat as his eyes narrowed. "A partnership is built on trust and truth, the kind you can stake your life on. I always thought we had that, but time changes a lot of things. With that in mind, I can't see any type of collaboration between us. If you successfully purchase the Trails' End, I'll surrender all interests I have in the ranch."

Her eyes grew even larger. Though he felt like a heel, he had to choose self-preservation or lose everything he'd worked for over the past ten years. "If I get the ranch, I'll expect the same courtesy."

⟪

She'd always loved walking the corridors of the hospital. Within this building, professionals used their skills to diagnose, treat and heal.

And where her father's patients were concerned, lots of prayer.

Jen punched the elevator call button and waited for the door to open. Never mind the elevator, she'd take the stairs. Spending the day meeting with specialists and reviewing files on all the new children coming to the camp on Saturday, meant a lot of sitting and waiting for the doctors to have a few moments to talk to her. As an oncology nurse, she recognized warning signs of the various infections that could flare, but not all of them. Before each camp session, she reviewed the charts and acquainted herself with the treatments. Be prepared wasn't just the Boy Scout motto. Knowing the extent of the treatments the children had endured to get to the point where they could attend camp, Jen didn't want anything to stand in the way of their fun.

Checking her watch, she picked up the pace heading toward the stairwell. Hours earlier, the morning sun had warmed her skin through her long sleeved t-shirt. If she acted fast, she might still get to enjoy part of the warm, fall day. She didn't like too much down time, but this last session was out of the ordinary she figured she'd better catch up on relax time before the next group arrived.

A voice at the end of the corridor made her slow and stop. Zac stood at the end of the lobby. It had been a week since they'd had their discussion and she'd been wondering if he'd made good on his promise. It wasn't like she could casually ask anyone at the clinic if he'd been in for a DNA swab without raising a few brows. He'd stopped to talk to a doctor at the edge of the hallway. A chill replaced thoughts of warm skin and beautiful days. She didn't have to wait for the man in the lab coat to turn to recognize him.

Zac was talking to her father.

A lump formed in her throat. All the years she'd protected her secret, guarded her heart, maintained poise. All those years of biting her nails thinking someone would find out, and now, her worst fears were playing out in front of her. Zac had to believe she hadn't shared the news with anyone - *anyone* -

including her father. Oh Lord, what was she going to say?

Her father turned as if she'd voiced her panic. He grinned and motioned her over. "Jen, look who's here. I haven't seen Zac in years. Did you know he was in town?"

Zac stiffened as she stepped up beside her father. He nodded to her, though the effort was clearly forced. She recognized every nuance of Zac Davidson's emotions, and at the moment, she knew his civility was sorely pressed.

"Dad, I've been all around the hospital this morning." She kissed his cheek. "You've been avoiding me."

"I've been working." He hugged her back and gestured toward Zac. "Zac tells me he's moving back to Hawk Ridge. Did you know that?"

"I've heard rumors."

"I don't know if Hawk Ridge is ready for you two to partner up again. Talk about a handful of trouble running around town." Her father laughed. "Oh, it definitely took a village to raise the two of you."

"Dad," she cautioned, trying to not make her diversion appear too obvious, "we're going to make Zac late for whatever appointment he has here at the clinic."

"That's right." Her dad folded his arms across his chest and nodded toward the reception area. "What can we do for you?"

The lump in her throat turned to molten thick lava, burning an acid trail all the way to her heart. She tried to catch Zac's eye, but he refused to glance her way. She was so screwed.

"Just a routine test. Nothing special." Zac appeared completely unaffected by the clinic. He shifted his weight as he indicated the hall leading to the lab. "Thought it might be a good time for a checkup. Actually, Jen's the one who brought it up."

Her cheeks warmed as their attention centered on her. Her father raised a brow as she scrambled for an answer to the question she knew he was about to ask. "Nothing's wrong, Dad. I was talking about cancer and the kids, and well, one thing led to another."

Her dad nodded and nudged Zac. "You'll have that, you know. Doctors and nurses. We just can't leave our work in the office."

"I've noticed that." Zac reached out and snagged her wrist, his touch light, yet firm. "Glad you showed up, Bean. Show me where I'm supposed to go."

He tugged her close and Jen could only offer a weak smile. "See ya, Dad."

"Glad to see you two still look out for one another. Just stay out of trouble." He shook his head and opened the folder he'd had tucked under his arm. Not bothering to look where he was going, her dad followed the familiar path to his office.

Jen drew a breath filling her senses with the warmest scent of clean, cotton shirt and male strength she'd ever imagined. She knew she needed to straighten and put distance between them, but her body refused to entertain the idea. She pressed her ear to his chest, the strong, steady heartbeat reminding her of summers past and almost making her forget the chill of the present. As Zac's arm clamped around her shoulders, drawing her close to his side, she wiggled out of his hold and stepped back, putting a couple of vinyl floor tiles between them. "Thanks for not telling my dad."

"Don't get the wrong idea of sparing feelings. I didn't think this was any of his business."

The tight, hostile edge to his voice caught her off guard. She'd never heard Zac refer to her father with anything but respect. She hadn't considered how Zac might want to handle the situation. Protecting her dad from her errors in judgment had been her primary focus. "The lab is right around the corner."

Just before they reached the lab, Zac took her hand and tugged her down an empty corridor with an emergency door at the end. "I hate going into situations blind. What's going to happen here? How long is this going to take? How am I supposed to answer their questions?"

The edge to his voice had faded. He sounded more like the Zac she knew years ago, the one who was always up for the adventure, but then turned to her for confirmation. Her dad was right. They still looked out for one another. "They're going to swab the inside of your cheeks to collect cells for tissue typing."

Goose bumps ran up her arm as the callous pad of his thumb traced a nervous path back and forth along the inside of her wrist. She placed her other hand over his knuckles. "I'm sorry I didn't explain this earlier. I didn't think you wanted to talk to me."

"I didn't." He squeezed her fingers. "But since you're here, I'm asking."

"I guess I deserve that." She relaxed a bit. She might stumble over farming and business plans, but nursing was her home turf. "The blood sample they'll collect is for the HLA - Human Leucocyte Antigen -

test. The antigen is a substance that acts like a marker, it's unique to you, much like your fingerprints." She released his hand and wiggled her fingers at him.

At his silence, she rubbed her eyebrows trying to think of a way to make her explanation make sense. "Your blood test - this HLA testing - uses a DNA based method to match patients and donors. We should know if you're a match in a week or two."

"That long? Does that give Carli enough time?"

"It should."

His gaze bore down on her and Jen didn't have the energy to remain upbeat. She covered his knuckles with her palm again and gave him a squeeze. "Look, I know you didn't want me to be here today or you would have invited me. I was just finishing up some medical background checks so I guess I'll go on back to the camp."

When she tried to pull back, he tightened his grip. "Don't go."

The soft words tugged at her heart. "You'll be fine."

"I know that." He loosened his hold, his fingers barely wrapped around hers. "I might need a translator-- you know, for all that medical-eze."

Jen understood. Fear of the unknown, especially of this caliber was enough to fell even the mightiest of cowboys. She nodded with practiced ease, as if encouraging a new patient to face the future with courage, even though Zac was no stranger and courage only came to her as a gift from God. She slipped her hand properly into his. A warm flush washed over her as she tugged him toward the open laboratory door. "I'll tell them you faint at the sight of blood."

« CHAPTER FIVE »

"Is Jennifer O'Reilly here?"

The brunette at the filing cabinet turned, her dark brown gaze assessing him from the top of his ball cap to the bottom of his boots. She frowned. Obviously, he didn't pass assessment. "And who may I ask is calling?"

"Zac Davidson."

She waited a moment as if expecting more from him. She'd only asked his name, that's all the information he was going to give her. She closed the filing drawer and stepped around the desk. "One moment, I'll see if she's available."

He'd stopped in to the health office as a courtesy to her and the camp. He needed to begin cutting hay in the final portion of fields and didn't want the kids scared by the equipment he planned to drive right through the middle of camp. The tractor looked in usable condition, he hoped the rake and baler shaped up, too. Right now, he needed the swather and from the brief glimpse he'd had of the machinery the day he pulled into the ranch, it looked like someone had upgraded their old one to a model with an enclosed cab. The cab was a luxury. Zac just hoped the thing ran.

"Zac." Jen came around the corner, his name floated off her lips with the same breathy sound he remembered from years ago. "Glad you dropped by. What can I do for you?"

Jeans, a yellow t-shirt and her hair pulled back into a mess of waves, Jen didn't look any different than the last time he'd seen her. He glanced between her, the woman he'd just spoken to, and a teenage girl sorting boxes in the corner of the room. They looked professional, she didn't. "Where's your coat?"

Jen blinked a couple of times. "You mean my lab coat? It's hanging on my chair. Why?"

Both the other women stared at him as if expecting an intelligent answer, too. Why did he have to say anything? He hadn't come for conversation. "Nothing."

"Tina and Michelle need pockets for stuff." She pointed to the bulges in their pockets. Waving her hand along her torso, she grinned with a sassy wink. "I'm a paper pusher. I don't do stuff."

"Didn't you say you're the director of the place?" He shifted his weight wishing he'd stopped at the doorway instead of barging mid-way into the room. "Don't you have to dress up?"

"This is summer camp. My business suit is at the back of my closet."

Her laugh warmed him like morning sun on a growing field. He ducked his head, feeling the heat intensify as the nurse closest to him continued to stare. He wouldn't have felt so foolish if the others hadn't been there. Oh well, it wasn't the last mistake he'd make in his lifetime. "I'll get it right next time. I came to tell you I'm cutting today. I need to drive through the compound to get to my field. I didn't want to scare the kids."

The gal to his side went back to filing and the teenager had lost interest a while back. With the pressure off, Zac squared his attention back on Jen. "You have a PA system around here to warn them?"

Jen glanced at her watch and frowned. "It's ten o'clock. I thought you hit the fields at the crack of dawn?"

"The hay was too wet. You've got to wait until the sun rises and warms before you can cut this late in the season." At her continued frown, he understood her confusion. "You better research that and put it in your report for the loan. It'll help your case if the committee thinks you know what you're doing."

Her smile faded. "I do know what I'm doing."

"I know that," he said, suddenly missing the banter. "But you've got to convince *them* of it if you have any hope of getting your loan."

Her eyes narrowed. "Why are you helping me?"

Good question. She'd blindsided him with the news of their child and his emotions still churned over her deception. Now this child was sick and she had to turn to him for help. His gut clenched at the realization that Jen saw him as a screw up, just like all the rest of the town. She hadn't even given him a chance to do the right thing all those years ago.

"Zac? Don't think too hard about it. I don't need your help." Crossing her arms, she struck a stance.

"Can't you drive around the property and enter through the other gates?"

Her curt words cut through his fog. Of course she didn't need his help. She never had. He'd just been fool enough to never notice. "I need to get to work," he ground out. If he shared his real opinion of their situation, he'd only be inviting censure. Right now, he was in a lose-lose position. He indicated the door. "Last time I looked, Jess Eklund still owned this property. He said "cut hay" so I'm cutting hay, and doing it as cost effectively as I can. I just stopped by to warn you about the equipment."

Her brows drew together tightly. He recognized that look and knew he hadn't had the last word in this matter. She slipped around him and took off at a good clip across the driveway toward the barn. Zac turned toward the equipment shed and crossed the grounds with long strides. Why had he bothered telling her in the first place? He should have just driven through the compound and let the staff run after the kids. She was probably headed over to cry on her camp minion's shoulder and tell him how mean the cowboy brute had been to her. What was was the guy's name? Zac frowned as he grabbed the door handle and opened the cab of the swather. Patrick? Patrick. That sounded right. He turned on the engine and shifted into gear. Easing off the clutch, he steered the machine around the health clinic and toward the barn. Patrick. Why did he care who she turned to? Whatever was between Zac and Jen at one time was now ancient history.

Except for the child. His child. The child she gave away without even telling him.

The sole of his boot kept the accelerator steady even as Zac fought the urge to gun the engine. Nothing would have brought greater satisfaction to him than ripping through the compound at full speed to put the entire scene behind him. He palmed the shift knob and reduced his speed as he drew closer to the open area by the playground. No sense in injuring innocent kids just to placate his mood.

As he rolled closer he saw Jen coming out of the barn with a child on either side of her. Behind her followed another dozen kids of varying ages and heights. What had she done? Rallied the troops to support her cause? Which one would throw the first stone? All of them waved as he drove up. His senses came alive as he slowed to a crawl, careful not to hit any of the children. If her plan was to send him to prison for hit-and-run so he wouldn't mess up her plans, she'd brainstormed the wrong idea.

He stopped and opened the door. "I told you I was coming through."

She gave him the universal sign to cut the engine as she nodded. He turned the key and the noise died. More kids swarmed out of the barn.

"Gather round, kids. This is Mr. Zac. He's here to cut the hay in the fields." Her smile tightened as she turned toward the children. "Have any of you ever seen a tractor?"

The kids stared wide-eyed, all of them shaking their heads. Zac knew what a goldfish felt like. The children gathered around him displayed varying stages of cancer recovery. A couple children had lost their hair; a few wore hats and gloves to protect their skin from the sun; one little girl huddled within the warm folds of a puffy down coat while another clutched the edges of her sweater together as if her life depended on it. He glanced over the crowd of children who had gone through a medical war and emerged on the other side.

"People come to the mountains to ski and hike and camp. It's beautiful up here for vacations and camps, right?"

"Right!" The kids answered as one voice, laughing and jumping up and down.

Jen raised her hand and the group went quiet. "God blessed this land to raise crops, too. Our growing season is much shorter than the plains, but we harvest hay and grains, too. Mr. Zac is going to cut hay so we have food for our horses and cattle this winter. He's going to drive through here over the next couple of weeks on different equipment to get his job done while we enjoy camp. He's going to keep an eye out for you, but we have to be careful not to get in his way."

"Mr. Zac?" A little girl with cast on her forearm waved from the back. "Can we have a ride?"

The kids all stared at him, eager smiles ranging from timid to rarin'-to-go. What was protocol for something like this? He stared at a nightmare liability case if anyone got hurt.

Jen held up her hand again and the group went quiet. "This camp session is the last one of the year because the days are getting short and the nights are colder. Mr. Zac has a lot of work to do before the snow falls. The soon he's gets done, the better." She angled her chin toward him with a hesitant smile. "Let's pray that he gets his work done in time, and maybe he'll have time to visit with us."

"Are you a real cowboy, Mr. Zac?" The little girl at the back had moved to the front. Her soft blonde curls clouded around her face. "Where's your cowboy hat?"

He preferred a ball cap. He hadn't had a haircut in a while so he didn't know what the wave in his hair had planned for the day. Besides, the ball cap was cooler in the summer than a hat. "What's your name, sweetheart?"

A bright pink colored her cheeks. "Amy."

"Well, Amy, when I'm driving a tractor with a cab, a hat gets in the way. I wear my cowboy hat when I ride my horse."

"We have horses here," -- she turned and looked at Jen -- "don't we, Miss Jennifer?"

Jen placed her hand on the girl's shoulder and gave her a hug. "Yes, we do, Amy. Maybe when Mr. Zac is finished in the fields, he'll come ride with us."

"Would you, Mr. Zac?"

Zac caught Jen's gaze, the sweet softness in her blue eyes taking him back years to the time they'd played at the Trails' End. They'd ridden horses, chased around the hay bales and kissed in the shadows like the summer would never end. The whole time, she made him feel special.

"Mr. Zac?" Amy stared expectantly as did the rest of the kids.

The memory faded but the warmth in his heart remained. He nodded. "I know some roping tricks, too."

(Q)

"This is ridiculous. He's driving farm equipment through the camp, working strange hours, interrupting our activities." Jen paced across the hard wood floor, turning at the elk mount above the oak bookcase and retracing her steps. "It's like he wants to destroy everything I've worked for and ruin what we're trying to do for the kids."

"Sit down before you hurt yourself." Trevor Hockett caught her by the shoulders and directed her to the club chair. He held on until she sank into the plush cushion. "Now, take a breath and douse the steam rising from your collar. Start again and tell me who *he* is."

Jen sat on the edge of the chair and crossed her legs. She managed a breath, but there was nothing deep about it. "Zac Davidson is running equipment across the compound at all times during the day. He goes from one field to another and each time I stop him, he tells me he's being economical. He doesn't want to waste gas and time."

"I can't believe Zac is putting the kids at risk like that." Trevor hiked a hip on the edge of his mahogany desk. Settling his chin in his palm, he tapped his finger along his jaw. "He's pretty ruthless in business deals, but I never thought he'd put a child in danger."

Her conscience slapped her. "He's not really putting the kids in danger. He stops by the rec center and tells us ahead of time that he's coming through so we can keep the kids out of the way."

"So he's not a hazard." He lowered his hand to the desk and leaned toward her. "What's the problem?"

Nothing...Everything. "He's a big, huge, irritating distraction, Trevor. We're trying to play soccer games, coach archery, play games outside while the temps are warm, and he's running haying equipment just past the trees. Can't he wait until this *final* camp session is over?"

Dressed in jeans and a white button down shirt, Trevor exuded the cowboy mystic with a lawyer's logic. He sat there staring at her as her face warmed, his booted foot swinging back and forth from the edge of the desk. Jen had never seen Trevor in action in the courtroom, but from the way he weighed his speculation of her reasons, she knew his defense would be nothing short of killer.

"Jen, pull your head out of the barn and think about what you're saying. Our days are short; the nights are chilly and longer." He ticked off the reasons on his fingers. "Time is running out on the harvest. He has to cut and bale while the weather permits."

"But we haven't heard any of the equipment while Splint and Max were working." She pointed out, defending her ire. "They worked at the other end of the property. We didn't even know they were there."

Trevor laid a look on her. "With our growing season up here, you cut fields once. If the guys cut and baled the far fields already, the ones left are the plots closer to the ranch house and the camp. Jen, Zac can only harvest what's left to harvest. If you haven't figured out the basics of farming, your business plan is going to sink."

Understanding dawned through her anger. Max had told her they'd try not to disrupt her camp session a couple of weeks ago, and she'd barely realized they'd been running equipment. Of course, they started in the far fields. Her palm itched to smack herself upside the head. Still, understanding the problem didn't make her feel better. She wasn't ready to concede. "This session is not giving the campers the full wilderness experience."

"I hate to say it, but that's not Zac's fault. Maybe you shouldn't schedule anything beyond Labor Day."

"Trevor." Her nails dug deeper into her palms as she glared at his raised brow. "Whose side are you on?"

"The side of common sense which seems to have been thrown completely into the ditch." He shook his head as he stood from his perch and angled around the desk. "What's gotten into you? You and Zac used to be inseparable, now you're tearing into him like a mother raccoon defending her stash."

She watched him settle into his chair and lean back. "Trevor, he wants my ranch. He's got Jess on his side, and between the two of them there's no telling what kind of loophole they're going to create." Jen spared no thought to the shallowness of her explanation. "Arthur and I had it all figured out. Jess is supposed to sell the ranch to *me*."

"The will states you get first chance at buying the ranch at the agreed upon price." He rested his elbows on the arms of the chair. "I'm not going to let anything mess with the stated wishes of that will. There are stipulations you have to meet before this deal will go through and you're well on your way to meeting them. There's nothing wrong with Jess accepting a back-up contract. It's only good business. Especially when the second offer comes from a local family with ties to the community. Jess has all angles sown up. He can't lose." Trevor splayed his hands and shrugged. "That's the way good business runs."

She couldn't believe her ears. "You're helping me get this deal, remember?"

"I can only help you as long as you help yourself, and fighting Zac Davidson over something he hasn't done is not smart thinking." He steepled his fingers and stared at her. "Again I ask, what's up between you and Zac?"

She couldn't tell him about Carli, or the tests, or the cancer. How was she supposed to explain her irrational behavior? *Oh Lord, I'm so confused.* "Too much stress," she mumbled.

"If you think you're stressed now, Jennifer O'Reilly, be prepared for ten times worse when you buy the Trails' End. If I were you, I'd make peace with Zac and get your head back on straight. Time is running out." He softened his tone and a measure of encouragement filled the room. "You only have a few more weeks to get your plans in place before your loan review. You'll be finishing up this camp session, completing your business plan and your planting schedule. Don't forget the Foundation and fund-raising. I'm counting on you to wow the committee with your brilliance."

He paused as the enormity of the situation washed over her. "Jen, I'm here for you."

All she wanted to do was dive into her bed, rub her face into her pillow and pull the covers up over her head. Her dream seemed so easy to attain when she and Arthur had talked about the barn and outbuildings being remodeled for a recovery camp. They'd exchanged ideas and drawn up plans while drinking iced tea on the porch of his old ranch house. No mention of crops, or equipment maintenance, or structural soundness had crossed her mind until after the good Lord had called Arthur home and Jess Eklund had to offer her first purchase rights as his father's will had dictated. Lucky for her, Trevor Hockett had drawn up Arthur's will. He was aware of

Arthur's enthusiasm for her project. Trevor had defended her claim, had assured Jess she could present an acceptable purchase proposal.

Right now, Jen feared the worst. "Trevor?"

"Hmm?"

"Do you really think I can do this?" She barely heard her own words.

"Yes." He stretched his arm across the desk and touched her hand with the tips of his fingers. "Yes, I do. But Jen? No amount of my faith in you will help if you don't have faith in yourself. Your heart has been knocked askew and needs to be put back in place. Remember, the kids come first. Grow God's faith in the kids He's entrusted to you. Show them how their weakness has only made them stronger. Put His work first and everything else will fall into place." A grin eased across his face. "Isn't that what you always told me?"

"You can't use my own logic against me."

"I certainly can. Junior High debate team told me so."

"Nerd." She laughed, despite the tension mounting in her shoulders.

He grinned "True, but I'm a nerd who believes that things happen for a reason. Believe this will work out for the best."

« CHAPTER SIX »

AMAZING HOW DARK THE nights got on the mountain without the lights of the city. Bright stars sparkled in nothing but inky black. An easy breeze rustled the limbs of the blue spruces making the light of the partial moon dance through their needles.

Zac walked along the dirt service road back to his truck parked by the storage shed. The feel of solid ground beneath his feet a relief from the jarring rhythm of the Eklund swather. Ancient workhorse. Zac rubbed the palm of his hand. The steering wheel rattled so hard, he wasn't sure the nerves in his palm would ever be the same.

He hadn't driven farm equipment since he'd left the Circle D twelve years earlier – the technique easily remembered; the sore muscles conveniently forgotten. Installing a hot tub with turbo jets jumped to the top of his must-have list.

"Isn't it late to be calling?"

Zac jerked toward the quiet voice coming from the shadows on the porch. Jen sat in the wicker loveseat on the other side of the porch, her feet tucked up in the cushions. She pulled the earphone and turned off her MP3 player. The other day they'd stood by the railing, each of them taking a turn pacing the porch as she revealed the details of her painful secret. Tonight, she looked as cozy and inviting as her gentle voice.

His gaze quickly adjusted to the light. Her tousled hair covering her shoulders kept him staring. "Didn't anyone tell you farmers put in long days?"

She straightened in her seat and brushed strands of hair from her face as if she'd been dozing. "How do you cut a field at night?"

"Headlights." He swallowed the sigh he felt as she stretched and settled back into the chair. Though he'd fortified walls against her in his mind, his heart summoned unappreciated memories of cold football games where they'd huddled together beneath a blanket in the stadium stands, her frigid hands tunneled within the folds of his jacket for warmth and his arm curled possessively around her shoulders making sure she stayed close. Every few plays she'd shift and stretch, his palms caressing the toned muscles of her shoulders before she settled back against him. He shook away the memory as vivid as if it were just last weekend. "Modern marvels."

"You've been working all afternoon and evening?" She yawned while she arranged the paperwork scattered around her. "Have you eaten anything?"

A civil conversation was the last thing he'd expected. Sarcastic and withering, yes; sleepy and inviting, no. With his boot on the bottom step of the porch, he leaned against the newel post. "That's what I'm heading to do. Eat and sleep. Then tomorrow, do it all again. I didn't mean to disturb you. I'll roll on home now."

"Zac, come up here and sit down. I've got leftovers." She stood and stretched her arms over her head. With the kinks worked out, she extended her hand to him like a lifeline. "C'mon. The Bible says to feed the hungry."

His palm slipped into hers, her skin warm and soft. He lumbered up the two steps like an ox. "I'm not a fan of leftovers."

"They're not leftovers to you." She pulled him toward the other wicker chair then let go. "I'll be right back."

Not an ounce of resistance remained in him. Zac sat down as the screen door closed behind Jennifer and the lights clicked on inside the house. A soft glow bathed over the porch. He tilted his head and caught the chirping of late season crickets in the distance. A mild breeze swept across the porch blowing the ragged ends of his hair on his collar and rustling the papers stacked on the side table.

He removed his ball cap and settled it on top of the pile. A few sheets sat stacked on the other chair beneath the MP3 player. Zac scooped up the papers and player, sticking an earbud into his ear and pressing play. A soft ballad of Chris LeDoux's sounded over the wire. He started to hum along with the familiar melody about the county fair while glancing over the papers.

Fund-raising prospects. Cattleman's Association. He sifted down the pile. Seeding information. Crop rotations. Yield to acre averages.

A quick grin tugged at his lips. She took this entire farmer thing to heart. Good for her. Showed tenacity. All good medical directors needed dedication to their jobs.

Only farming wasn't really in her job description.

The screen door creaked open and the fragrant scent of pasta sauce rode the breeze. His mouth watered as he identified cheese and sausage, too.

"Noodle-roni and garlic bread." She stopped beside him with a bowl in one hand and a plate in the other. "Like I said, it's not much, but I warmed it fast."

"Mmm, smells like you slaved all day." The aroma of garlic and tomato lassoed his fragmented attention. He angled towards her, vowing not to let a morsel go to waste.

"Flattery will get you nowhere. The good Lord wouldn't have forgiven me if I'd sat back in silence as one of His hungry urchins crossed my path."

Zac chuckled as he set down her work and accepted the dish. "Nothing like a late night dinner shared with fr--." He stopped before the word slipped out. "Shared. A meal shared."

Her silence sent a fission of warning down his spine. They'd drawn their prospective lines and she held fast. He would've too if his stomach hadn't growled. What was the saying about women waging war with food as their weapon of choice? He positioned the plate on his lap and bowed his head. "Thank you, Lord for this sustaining meal offered in truce." He opened his one eye and looked up at her.

One side of her mouth angled up and a tiny dimple creased her cheek. Lucky him. "Amen."

He picked up his fork and shoveled in a bite. A moan of pleasure almost escaped over the simple blend of tomato sauce, sausage and cheese. "So, how was your day?"

Her smile faded and a line appeared across her forehead. She glanced around at the papers on the furniture and then to the door. "No need for small talk. I'm glad I could help you out before you starved. I'll pick up and give you some peace."

He swallowed too quickly and had to stifle a choke. He didn't want her to leave, not yet. Nodding toward the seat she'd recently vacated, he caught her wary gaze. "C'mon, Jen. If you don't keep me company, I'll eat too fast and then have indigestion all night. You wouldn't want that on your conscience."

A brow shot up and he cleared his throat. "Or then, maybe you would."

Obviously torn between running into the house and staying outside, she stood still a moment longer before reaching over his plate and tugging the earbud out of his ear. She rolled up the wires and gathered her player. "I wondered where I'd set that down." Placing the player atop the stack of papers, she stepped around the table and sat down. "Now, what were you saying about my wishing you ill?"

"Nothing. Nothing at all." He took a forkful of noodles, chewed and swallowed.

Her knee brushed his as she crossed her legs causing a jolt of awareness to race through his veins. Funny how vulnerable folks got when suffering sleep deprivation. He focused on eating.

She combed her fingers through the tousled mass of blonde hair, a few strands refusing to cooperate. "Our schedule is filling up for next year, which is a good thing. Have to make every penny count when you're a non-profit. But the best part is watching the kids play and regain the confidence they once had. Going through cancer treatments changes people. Now that they've finished and the enemy is at bay, they have a safe, fun place to celebrate. I love everything we're able to do here."

Zac listened to the contentment in her voice that mirrored her words. Jennifer had always known what she wanted out of life and now she lived her dream. After all these years, he'd finally discovered what he wanted in life and was reaching out to grab it, too. Unfortunately, both their dreams ended in the same place and only one would win the prize.

The harshness of reality bit at his own contentment. He never thought he'd be at such life-altering odds with Jennifer O'Reilly. They'd shared so much in their youth; little wonder they'd remain roped together as adults. "So, this little girl -- Carli. If she doesn't find a match, what will happen?"

At her sharp intake of air, Zac knew he'd just leveled their playing field.

"They have some time. I'm not an expert in leukemia treatment, but I know if the treatment was urgent, they wouldn't have bothered with attorneys sending letters. The adoption service would have contacted me immediately since I allowed for open medical records."

"And they asked you to ferret out other possible donors without background checks or anything?" He'd kept his tone light and inquisitive, taking a bite of garlic bread to emphasize his detachment to the situation.

"I knew your blood type, that's a good place to start," she replied.

"You know my blood type?" Scooping up the last of the crusty cheese on the heel of the garlic bread, he popped the end of his dinner in his mouth.

"I was a nurse at the Hawk Ridge clinic for a time, remember?" Her fingers played with the bottom edge of her t-shirt. "My dad helped deliver you. Your records go back a long way."

The mouth-watering food in his mouth turned tasteless in a heartbeat. "Your dad gave you access to my medical records? You knew what you were looking for, right? You could have pegged me as a donor match without the paternity angle." His fingers gripped the plate to keep his voice steady. "Why didn't you just ask me to help instead of beating around the subject...making it sound like a lie?"

"I didn't lie." She twisted in her seat, and the frown deepened across her forehead. "You and I had a daughter, Isaac Davidson. A healthy, 6 pound-8 ounce baby girl. A baby I never held, or even saw. I heard her though. A healthy lung-busting scream as her warm, cushioned world washed her out into reality." Her breath came in short bursts as she scooted to the edge of her seat. "My dad never found out. I don't want him to ever find out. He'd be hurt and disappointed."

"That's all well and good from your perspective, but remember, there was another family involved, too. Mine." All fragments of fatigue fell away as he met her nose to nose. "Don't you think this situation affected them, too?"

Her chin trembled as the muscles in her jaw clenched. "Not as badly as tearing my dad apart. He expected a lot from me."

"And mine didn't?"

"Zac, you marched to your own tune and dragged me along for the ride. Your family would have been shocked, but still would have rallied around you." On the edge of tears, she drew a ragged breath. "My dad would have blamed himself and wondered where he'd failed. Wondering why hadn't I held out for the real deal?"

"That is a pile, and you know it. We were going to marry, wasn't that proof enough?

Her watery eyes widened. "Marry? When did we ever discuss marriage? You never even told me you loved me."

"Of course I loved you, couldn't you tell?"

Her fist slammed down on the cushion. "Couldn't I tell?" Her voice cracked despite the laser glare she kept honed on him. "Zac, I wasn't about to assume anything like that. If you loved me, you would've told me. I waited for the words even as we," her gaze darted to her hands, her fingers twisting together, "even as we shared the most loving moment of my life, I never heard the *I love you*."

Zac slid his plate onto the table, conscious of her shoulders shaking and the small catch in her breath. He replayed the night, his mind flitting across every incredible moment. "I told you I loved you."

"I waited. I wished." She looked up, her eyes shining with tears that threatened to spill. "I heard you tell me you never wanted this moment to end. And then you kissed me and held me, but you never told me you loved me."

Just the two of them...the night he discovered what loving someone meant. All the tender feelings he'd held for Jen rushed back. His best friend. His buddy. His girl. Hadn't she known he'd exposed his heart to her that night? She'd wanted words? How was he supposed to know that? He'd loved her. He thought she loved him back. "I lived for the moment. You knew me better than anyone."

"You're right." She lowered her voice. "I knew what we shared was real at the moment. But then, it was gone." She stood and took his plate, her hands trembling as she fingered the silverware. "That's all I had to base the decision I made for another human being's life. I never would have made you marry me."

He reached out and hooked a finger in the loop of her jeans. She stilled at his slight tug. His throat tightened, but he had to know. "Did you love me?"

Her muscles stiffened. She nodded.

"Would you have married me if I'd asked you?"

Her gaze trailed along his arm, across his shoulder and locked with his. She blinked as a small twitch worked at the corner of her mouth. "I never would've held you back."

« CHAPTER SEVEN »

Think of the kids.
Go beyond the expected.
Be gracious.

Jen pulled into the Circle D lot and cut the engine. Staring out her windshield, she deepened her breathing, trying to tamp down her frustration. That evening after seeing Trevor, she'd taken his advice when she saw Zac bone tired and invited him to eat and talk on her porch, and look what it got her -- a torn scab off a raw wound in her heart. She'd tried to be gracious; she'd tried to put the past behind her. All she'd succeeded in doing was wounding Zac just as deeply as the hurt ran in her.

Now, two days later, she still couldn't stop the tears from welling in her eyes. Wiping her eyes, she studied the early fall change in the fields and mountains in front of her. Autumn gold spread beyond the split rail fencing the color of the fields growing lighter the closer it got to the crest of the hills. Just beyond the pastures, mountains rose in jagged peaks, the bare rock waiting for a dusting of snow. Instead of peace filling her heart at the beautiful sight, all she wanted to do was cry.

She pinched between her brows and closed her eyes. *Lord, what's wrong with me? Why am I stabbing at Zac? Why can't I just ignore his pokes and be happy he's agreed to help Carli?*

Jen sat in her truck refusing to let the tears fall. She'd had no choice twelve years ago. Her daughter had a better life than she could've given her. She and Zac lived their lives exactly as they wanted to.

She'd done the right thing. She'd done the right thing. She'd done the right thing.

Slamming the palm of her free hand on the steering wheel, Jen released her pinch and opened her eyes. Zac had moved on; she'd been left to deal with the pregnancy by herself; she'd couldn't have faced her father, knowing how disappointed in her he would've been. All her reasons remained as solid as the day she'd decided she knew what was best for the baby. Zac had no right to judge her.

Wiping her eyes, she shoved the door open, grabbed her folder and slid out of the truck. No regrets. The past remained behind her, and she needed to look to the future. A future of sharing love and hope with those who needed it most.

"Jennifer, there you are. We were wondering if you were going to make it this morning." Grace Davidson stood on the back porch wiping a coffee mug with a dish towel. "C'mon in, I just set a pot to brewin'."

Jen forced a smile and once in place, relief spread through her. Grace had always been like a mother to her. She loved Grace -- no matter what her son was up to. "Great. I'm up for coffee anytime."

"And my apple crisp? Gabe just got back from Grand Junction with a couple of bushels of apples. Couldn't wait to bake with them."

The aroma gave away the treat even if Grace hadn't said anything about it. Jen followed her through the door and into the kitchen. "Martin, you're looking fit this morning." Jen hooked her purse strap over the coat hook.

Martin Davidson sat at the oak kitchen table, a pair of tortoise-shell reading glasses perched on the bridge of his nose and a copy of *Cattlemen's Quarterly* open beneath the heel of his sturdy palm. "Jennifer, glad you made it. I was about to head to the shop. Thought you'd forgotten about us."

"Never. Sorry I'm late." She'd been waiting for Zac to show up and get to work before she left. Zac never showed and she couldn't wait any longer. She prayed the whole way over she wouldn't pass him on the road. "Especially when I need your advice so badly. Thanks for looking over my business plan."

"Seems to me you're doing a fine job yourself." Martin lifted his cup and winced after taking a swallow. "I'll never get used to tea."

"Coffee helped get you your heart attack. One cup a day is what Doc O'Reilly says. I turn a blind eye on the second cup you sneak after supper." Grace winked at Jen. "Now don't go telling your dad that."

"I'd never tattle. I love you guys too much." Warmth swelled through her simply acknowledging how much the Davidsons meant to her. They'd been there for her when her mother died and wrapped her and her brother in support, especially when her dad grieved in his own way--a way that didn't include comforting his own children. "Not to worry. Dad builds fudge factor into his directions."

Grace laughed. "Always good to have a medical expert in the family." She gave Jen a sideways glance. "I had hopes we'd get one, too. That Zac let a real peach slip through his hands when he let you go. Funny, the way you two got along, I thought he'd be the first to get married and give us babies. Never thought our first grandchildren would come from Gabe."

What about my family? Acid burned in her belly as Zac's words from a few evenings back plagued her. His family. The family that loved her, too. Jen ground her teeth as her conscience tore at her heart. *Why now, Lord? Why is everything erupting around me now?* The longing in Grace's voice made Jen want to cry. Over the past couple of days, everything made her cry.

Maybe that's what she needed. A good dam-buster of a cry. Get it all out of her system, then maybe she'd deal with the camp, the ranch, the possible transplant. She folded her hands on her lap to keep them from shaking. *Lord, help me keep it together, just for a little while longer.*

Martin scooped up the folder Jen had set on the table and flipped through her papers. "Mellie's doing a good job of catching up. A grandson she raised proper and a pair of granddaughters on the way. Count your blessings Grace, not your years." He pulled out the sheet of graph paper she'd redrawn her boundaries on. "Looks pretty true to life here,

Jennifer. Glad you thought to look at the lay of the land instead of just going off of the record maps. Topography changes over time. They'll be making their own revisions," -- he held up the sheet and shook it -- "but seeing you beat them to it will make the surveyors, and the loan folks, pretty happy."

Martin's praise only made her stomach hurt worse. She wouldn't have thought of it if Zac hadn't mentioned the boundary discrepancies to her. "Zac pointed that out to me the other day."

"Makes sense he'd want you to get it right. No one loves that land more than Zac, and no one knows it better." He shuffled the papers together with the budget page on top. "Arthur Eklund did a good thing when he wrote you into his will, Jennifer. That ranch needs a loving touch and a useful purpose. It hasn't been farmed to its potential in years. It'll be rough going at first, but with a good crop plan and solid funding for that camp, you'll be on top of things in no time." He tapped on the sheet. "Now, looks like we've got to get more realistic with these numbers. Just because Eklund guaranteed a below market price for you, doesn't mean the deal is sealed. Nothing drives the money guys crazier than an application with pie in the sky figures. We'll work this through then have Zac look at it."

Zac? "I don't want to bother him. He's got enough on his mind already." *More than you'll know.*

"Never you mind Zac's time." Martin gave her the one eye over the top of his glasses. "The Circle D pays him to be on top of our numbers. It's in the best interest of the Circle D that we have good neighbors. The Trails' End used to be part of the Circle D, you know."

Grace leaned her hip against the table and sighed. "That place used to scare the goodness out of me. Zac spent so much time out there exploring the caves and mine shafts with Jess, I was certain they'd fall into one. Oh my, oh my. I prayed up a storm for the good Lord to send a legion of angels to watch over those boys."

"I don't remember Kade ever mentioning the caves." Happy memories of the three of them exploring anything that came their way wove through her mind. The mention of Jess shot her thoughts to dust. "Zac didn't either."

"Zac spent less time over at the Trails' End when we took you and your brother in while your dad took care of your mom. Kade and Zac began roping together during that time and he only went over to the Trails' End when Jess called."

Grace slid a steaming cup of coffee in front of Jen and laughed. "I remember the scuffed up hands when the boys decided they wanted to make a go of the roping. I didn't think Kade would have any fingers left. That rope took its measure of skin."

Martin chuckled and laid the papers down. "Yep, good for the boys. They learned to keep their fingers and thumbs tucked in close."

Jen gave Martin a half-hearted grin. Zac learned to nimbly keep his hands in one piece. A skill he aptly applied to more facets of his life that included protecting his heart while leaving a trail of shattered dreams behind him.

Jen grabbed the mug and took a careful sip. She indicated the papers as she set the coffee back down. "Martin, where do we start?"

"Hand me the breaker bar."

Zac grabbed the long bar from the bench and placed the end in Gabe's open palm. "Why'd you crank these bolts down so tight?"

"Guess I didn't know my own strength." Gabe shot Zac a look before fitting the socket into place. With the added length, he gripped the handle and pulled a couple of times until the nut broke free. "Shouldn't you be haying your own place instead helping me change the blades on my equipment?"

Ignoring the sarcasm, Zac picked the nut from the ground and dropped it into the tool box drawer. "I'm trying to work a deal here. I help you, you help me. I can't sit on Eklund's equipment for another minute. The things rattle around the fields until I can't stand straight anymore. I need to use one of our swathers." Zac glanced past the line of engine parts and replacement fittings neatly stacked on shelves. His cousin, Hank and their barn manager Manny, could tear apart anything broken and fix it better than new with the proverbial baling twine and fence wire. Or course, having the right parts was always a plus.

He looked out the window of the barn at the equipment yard and spotted their old John Deere. "How about Ernie?"

"Are you crazy? We've got our own fields to cut, I need all the equipment the Circle D has running." Gabe broke another nut free. "Besides, I like driving Ernie. Good machine; dependable." He fit the socket around another nut. "Start thinking like a responsible rancher, Zac. Go buy your own equipment."

"After harvest. Right now, I have to work any angle possible to retain the ability to sit still."

Gabe laughed as he handed Zac another nut. "Sitting is highly overrated."

"I'll be the judge of that." Zac tossed it in the tool box and helped Gabe reach the next set of blades. "Speaking of aching muscles, how's Melanie doing? She looked pretty tired the other night."

"Good days and bad. Glad we're not in the heat of the summer. She tends to get a bit cranky when it's hot. Hand me another blade."

Zac did as he was asked. "She sounds excited about having twins."

"Yeah, after raising Jason by herself while finishing school, she says looking after two babies at one time will be a piece of cake. Mel and Mom have made more plans than I can listen to. Dad, Jason and I spend a lot of time out here in the barn while they're talking colors and cribs and all sorts of other stuff."

Zac stared at the blade Gabe eased in place. "Jason fits right in, doesn't he?"

"I love the kid. He's smart and funny. I'm proud to call him my son."

"You've adopted him?"

"When the twins are born, we'll be one big happy family."

One big happy family. Zac resisted the impending snort. Jennifer didn't think enough of him to share her life. It hadn't been easy for twenty-something Melanie to raise her son alone, but she did it. If something matters enough, you make it work. Obviously, being part of a family didn't matter to Jen. She chose the easy way out.

"Zac!"

"What?"

"If you're going to stand there, hand me the wrench. I can't fasten the blade back in place without it."

Zac glanced at the line of turtles still needed to have blades changed on the head. He hated changing blades. Tore open more jeans at the knee while working on them than he could count. He handed off the tool and stepped back. "Hurry up and show me what I can drive so my backside doesn't feel whooped."

Gabe gave the nut a final shove, laid the wrench on the ground beside the next set and stood up. "You know you've probably only got a good two weeks before the snow flies, and that's pushing it."

"Not a problem. Jess had Max cutting the lower belt and Splint's raking the rows. With the proper equipment, I shouldn't have much of a problem finishing up in a few days." He slapped the dirt from his jeans as they walked toward the door. "That's a lot of hay to bring in, but we'll do it. Nothing like seeing the crop put the ranch in the black."

Gabe reached for the door handle. "Is it true you have a back-up contract on the place?"

"It's just a back-up contract. There is a chance Jen won't meet the criteria and the sale will open up again. I don't want the Trails' End falling into an outsider's hands."

"Does 'outsider' include Jennifer O'Reilly?"

The joy of anticipating a good harvest turned sour at the mention of her name. "Last time I looked, she wasn't a Davidson."

"The last time you looked, Jen was a teenager."

Zac didn't want to revisit the argument. He'd had enough of that a few nights ago. Jen had been honest, she'd made it clear she hadn't wanted to marry him. That truth stung, but not anything he couldn't get over. They'd been an item, now they weren't. What more did she want from him?

A cool draft through the barn reminded him nice weather was running short. Great day to be working and what was he doing? Wasting time convincing his brother to loan him equipment. The angry thought evaporated as soon as the words gelled in his brain. He'd spent an hour talking with Gabe -- alone -- a feat he'd not been able to accomplish in all the days he'd been home without Grace or Martin inviting themselves into the conversation. He loved his folks, but it was nice not having someone tell him what to do. Gabe tended to listen, letting folks come to their conclusions.

Zac smacked his brother on the shoulder and indicated the door. "Let's go out and see what equipment you can spare. I'd like to get the job done while the sun's still shining."

"Patience, little brother." Gabe eased the door open and ambled through it like a stroll along a mountain trail. "Besides, anything I can spare will probably, at the very least, need an oil change. Let's look things over."

Zac shook his head, amazed Gabe ever got anything done. "Make hay while the sun's still shining," he muttered.

Gabe laughed. "Yeah, something like that."

They stepped through the barn door and squinted at the bright sunshine. It took a moment for his eyes to adjust as he looked across the corrals. His mom and dad stood next to the gate with Melanie laughing beside them. Right next to her stood Jennifer, her slim figure a dramatic contrast to Melanie's well-rounded form.

Not the only contrast he'd noticed recently. Melanie grabbed whatever the world shot at her and worked the situations until they shined despite the gloom surrounding her. She'd kept her child, not caring what anyone thought of her. She accepted the consequences and God blessed her for her faithfulness.

I never would've held you back. Jen's words mocked him with their double-edged meaning.

All those years he'd read Jen wrong. He'd imagined the noble in her, not realizing she'd supported him at her convenience, biding her time until he left.

He'd read her wrong before. It wouldn't happen again.

«CHAPTER EIGHT»

"Do my shoes match?"

Melanie waddled up to them as Jen stood by the corral fence with Grace and Martin. Slip-on shoes had replaced the hiking boots covering tanned feet and swollen ankles. "The shoes are fine, but you need to prop those feet up before your ankles burst."

Melanie twisted one way, and then the other trying to view her ankles. "I thought I heard sloshing, but hey, who'da thought it would be me?"

Her throaty laugh infected them all and Jen relaxed. Melanie had a problem with edema, a medical condition common to pregnant women, but knew enough to take care of it. Martin gave Mel a hug and helped her sit on the edge of a hay bunk that hadn't been moved into the corral yet. Jen knelt down and inspected the ankles in question, satisfied the puffy, yet firm flesh wasn't a warning. Drawn into the joy and expectancy of the birth due in the next few weeks, she laughed at the jokes Melanie pointed at herself. She'd liked Melanie from the moment she showed up in town and gave thanks to God that someone had finally saved Gabe from his workaholic self.

"The gals are all worked up today." She rubbed her belly as if trying to comfort the babies. "Grace, I have a feeling raising those three boys of yours was a cake walk compared to what I'm in for."

Memories of her own pregnancy engulfed her as Jen fought to bite her tongue. She'd lasted the entire nine months without sharing the experience with her family. The first flutter deep within her womb; the first time she saw a little elbow poke at her belly. The first contractions signaling her daughter was ready to meet the world.

Using the laughter of the moment to camouflage her watery eyes, she looked up and spied Gabe and Zac coming out of the barn. She met Zac's gaze and all of a sudden she wanted to share the months of her pregnancy with him, to wipe away the loneliness in her soul and replace it with the joyful miracle of life. He held her gaze as he drew closer, the boyish face of twelve year ago replaced by a handsome ruggedness and a curious dose of maturity. The intensity of his gaze bored through her with the power of a magnetic resonance imaging machine. Jen turned back, forced a chuckle at her continuing story as she tried to collect her scattered wits. Was she so distraught over the thought of babies and family and sickness and health, she'd begun hallucinating a happily ever after with the only person she'd made certain she could never have it with? What did she see in Zac's eyes? Remorse? Forgiveness? Love?

More like anger, hurt...resentment.

"Boys, about time you emerged from the barn," Martin called as he waved them over. "I'm the luckiest man alive surrounded by these beauties."

"You're a lucky man, Dad, but I hate to burst your bubble." Gabe came around and wrapped his arm around his wife's shoulders. "This beauty is mine."

Melanie grinned. "There's enough of me to go around."

"No way. You're mine, all mine." He bent over and kissed her ear earning a squeal from Melanie. "Dad's got his hands full with Mom."

"Don't I know it." Martin gave Grace an affectionate squeeze. "Kept me in line all these years whether I liked it or not."

"Oh, go on." Grace bumped Martin with her elbow, glowing at his attention. "You thought you could get away from me with that heart attack, but the good Lord had other plans. You're stuck with me, Martin Davidson, till death do us part...'almost' doesn't count."

Jen pasted on a smile, conscious of Zac standing beside her and the happy couples in front of them. Her emotions of moments earlier had run her ragged. She didn't know how to overcome the awkward feelings. "I can't think of two more perfect couples around."

Distance opened between them as he took a step back. A chasm grew, one that deepened with each chance encounter.

"And where exactly does that leave Bean? At the moment, she's young enough not to be set in her ways as some of our more mature beauties." He raised at brow at his mother. "Nor does she threaten to eat the community of Hawk Ridge out of house and home like the newest filly in the field." He winked at Melanie as she pursed her lips in mock offense. "Jen here is pretty much the dark horse of this race. Don't really know what to expect from her."

She hadn't a clue what he was talking about, but she recognized a diss when she heard one, didn't matter she didn't understood his jab. "Seems to me the stallion of the herd stands alone in his majesty," she bowed to Martin, "and the stalwart guard commands his post well." She nodded to Gabe with a smile. "So I guess that leaves the young colt of the bunch to gallop here and there, packing too much buck for his own good. Heaven only knows what will become of him."

Gabe clapped laughed, tipping his hat to her. "Well said, our dark horse. Looks like you pegged our wayward colt of the herd."

"Ahh, Gracie girl, what's this world coming to?" Martin rubbed his nose along the neckline of Grace's shirt and gave her a hug. "Goes to show how wisdom is wasted on the young."

"I couldn't agree more." Gabe moved behind Melanie and began kneading the muscles in her shoulders. "A lot more than wisdom was wasted on Zac. Surprised he turned out as well as he did for as ornery as he was."

Zac stepped up, hands on hips and shoulders squared. "Speak for yourself." He pointed at his dad. "Who do you think I used as a role model?"

Without skipping a beat, Grace, Martin and Gabe chimed in. "Great-grandpa Jeb."

"Who?" Melanie stretched her neck for Gabe to rub as she looked at Jen for answers.

"Second generation Davidson to own the Circle D," Jen filled in with a stage whisper.

"I am not GG Jeb." Zac scowled.

"Course not, son. But if anyone followed in his footsteps, it would be you." Martin shrugged. "Nothing wrong with that. It's all in the family. You've got a great mind for numbers and all, and no one could count cards better than Jeb. Too bad he apparently lost count during that one game of poker, but otherwise, legend has it, he made enough off of his games of chance to pay off the Circle D."

"What game did he lose?" Melanie reached up and stilled Gabe's working fingers.

Gabe pulled out of her grip and cupped her shoulders until Melanie relaxed back against his chest. "The last hand of the poker game he and Efrain Eklund played at the High Spring Saloon in town. Rumor had it Jeb Davidson pushed in all his chips and the deed to the Trails' End thinking he had the upper hand. When the dealer called the hand, Jeb laid down a full house, jacks high and nearly keeled over of apoplexy when ol' Efrain fanned out a flush, aces high."

"No. You're kidding right?" Apparently content after the massage, Melanie folded her hands across her bulging belly and looked around at the solemn faces. "But, you still own the Circle D."

Martin shrugged and showed four fingers. "When the Davidsons first homesteaded in Hawk Ridge, the Circle D was actually four different spreads - a ranch for each brother. After Jeb, the youngest brother, lost Trails' End, he came to live with George, the oldest brother. All the brothers got together and decided to unite the remaining property so it wouldn't be splintered apart. They consolidated so no one person could sell off any part of the acreage. The brothers named the one big spread the Circle D."

"So you're saying Jeb was the youngest of the Davidson boys much like Zac is the youngest now?" Jen tapped her finger against her chin making a great show of pondering. "I'm beginning to see the correlation. I didn't realize devil-may-care ran in the family genes."

"If there's a part of me similar to GG Jeb," Zac defended, his voice low. "It's that neither of us are afraid to take chances. Yes, the chance he took cost him dearly, but look at it this way, if GG hadn't lost the ranch, there wouldn't be a Circle D now. Who knows if we'd be here at all? You call GG irresponsible, but as far as I'm concerned, he made the Circle D the ranch it is today."

"Well said, son. I don't think I've heard Great Grandpa Jeb revered as an innovator, but you make a good case for it." Martin laughed. "And you've done well with the investment assets of the Circle D, too. If Jeb were alive today, he'd be proud to be compared to you."

"I'm not finished yet, either." Zac turned and looked Jen square in the eye. "Folks are always saying history repeats itself. How about history repairing itself? You never know how life will shake out."

Jen swallowed. Zac was bringing out the big guns now and she didn't want to start World War Three right here in the middle of a mountain corral. "You never know--" her words faltered as Zac pulled out his cell phone and frowned. He looked up and squinted into the sky as he angled away from his family to answer the call. "--what life...has...in store," she finished her sentence as Zac paced toward the corral gate.

Melanie twisted around and watched him walk away. "Looks serious, doesn't it?"

"He's been away from the office." Martin tilted his head back and speculated with his arms crossed over his chest. "His assistant is good, but Diane can't handle everything."

Gabe quirked his lips. "Maybe he forgot to file the quarterlies and the IRS is looking for him."

Grace waved him off. "That's not funny, Gabriel. He works on the company accounts at night, and usually has something for me to mail off in the morning."

Zac leaned against the fence panel, his shirt stretched taut over his shoulders. Jen tried to swallow the ball of guilt lodged in her throat. He worked at the Trails' End during the day and kept up with his financial responsibilities to Davidson Enterprises at night. No wonder he looked worn out...and all she'd done was add to his burdens. She shouldn't have lashed out at him. He'd had every right to be skeptical the day she told him about Carli.

The reality of the present interlaced with the past in her mind. Wasn't that why she'd never told him about her pregnancy to begin with? She hadn't wanted to burden him, to be the one responsible for stealing his dreams. Twelve years later, she'd managed to do it anyway.

Zac hung his head as he stuffed his phone in his back pocket. Jen's heart pounded as he turned on his heel and approached them, his swagger a bit slower, but still a hundred percent cowboy.

"Isaac, is something wrong?" A frown burrowed between her brows as Grace stared at her son.

He practically angled Jen out of the conversation as he flashed his mother a quick grin. "Nothing I can't handle. But it looks like I'll have drive to Denver in the morning to take care of a couple of things."

The creases at the corners of his eyes deepened and Jen knew something was up. She'd been stonewalled by that two-faced expression before. Unfortunately, he didn't give her time to figure it out.

"Let's go look at that John Deere you were going to loan me," Zac said to Gabe as he started off toward the equipment.

Gabe sighed and kissed the top of Melanie's head as he took off after his brother.

Jen watched Zac trudge across the lot, his slow steps a dead giveaway that what he needed to "handle" was more than nothing.

Tomorrow morning.

« CHAPTER NINE »

Fluorescent lights hummed overhead while Toby Keith sang a chirpy ballad about a big, blue note through the speaker embedded in the ceiling one table over. At 3:30 in the morning, Jennifer sat in a window booth of The Wildflower diner and stared out at the night sky that looked as black as the cup of coffee Sandy Kithcart set down in front of her, counting on the brew to keep her wits together. She flicked the laminated menu across her fingertips as her high school friend placed a hand towel on the table and swiped the surface clean.

"Can't say I expected anyone besides truckers to stop in this time of night, Jen." Sandy sounded bubbly despite the hour. "What's keeping you up?"

"A hunch." She took a sip of the coffee - freshly brewed and potent - before reaching for the creamer. "I'm hoping an old friend didn't break too many of his habits."

Nodding as if she understood, Sandy tossed the towel into a nearby tub. "You're secret's safe with me. I know how hard it is to keep private matters quiet in this town. Word gets out and spreads like wildfire, especially if it's juicy."

Jen almost choked as Sandy nudged her. She set down her coffee cup and wiped her mouth. "It's nothing like that. I've been busy with the camp and Zac's been, well, just busy. I wanted to catch him before he left to pick up some supplies this morning."

"You and Zac Davidson again, huh? I knew what you guys had in high school was real. Pam and Mary didn't believe me when I told them I thought you guys would make it. See? Wait until they hear--"

"Sandy," Jen cut in, grabbing her friend's arm like a lifeline. "You just promised you wouldn't tell anyone I was here, remember?"

"I'm not going to tell them *now*, silly goose. But I will eventually. Like at your wedding." Sandy patted Jen on the back. "I'll be right there reminding them I knew it all along."

"Well, don't be too hasty." Jen tried to sound calm as her heart pounded in her chest. After she and Zac had left the Circle D yesterday afternoon, they went to her house and called her friend at the lab. An opening was available, so they set up additional testing for today in Denver. She started talking about scheduling the tests and he'd made it plain he didn't want her to tag along.

"This isn't what you think," Jen blurted out before Sandy could embellish her imaginary situation more. "Zac and I aren't the same people we were in high school. We've gone separate ways. I just want to catch up over coffee. We're just friends."

"We'll see." She looked up as headlights pulled into the dimly lit parking lot. "Looks like your *friend* is here."

Jen drew a breath as she watched Zac get out of his truck and slam the door behind him. His black Carhartt jacket hugged his shoulders, the cuffs of his sleeves hanging loose as always. Dark jeans encased his long legs down to the extra length of denim at his boots. Zac Davidson turned heads when he casually walked down the street; when he dressed with purpose, the man was knock-down handsome. He opened the door to the diner and stepped into the lighted room, his dark hair curled out from under his ball cap giving him a boyish look that brought back high school all over again. He glanced up and down the counter and then around the room, his gaze stopped when he spotted her. Immediately the carefree look disappeared, replaced with a scowl.

He didn't wait for Sandy to seat him, he walked over and slid across from Jen in her booth.

"Mighty early for breakfast, isn't it?"

"Not for you." She searched his face for any sign of regret. All she saw was suspicion. "I was hoping you hadn't changed your ways too much. I remember too many drives to Denver with you that had to start with breakfast at the 'Flower."

"I'll have to rethink my habits." His long lashes brushed over his chilled cheeks in an extra-long blink. "What are you doing here? I told you I could do this myself."

"I know you can, Zac. I just want to help."

He propped his elbows on the table and leaned forward. "If you really want to help me, stay here and cut Eklund's fields. This dry weather isn't going to hold forever. I don't really have the time to be spending a day in Denver." His voice was low as he linked his fingers together.

That was no understatement. She had the Foundation coming for an inspection tomorrow and her reporting files were a mess. Patrick and Tina did their best to cover for her, but if she was going to be named director of the camp by the Foundation, she was going to have to make the presentation tomorrow, not her staff. If the good Lord smiled on her and gave them the best case scenario at the medical center, they'd be back in Hawk Ridge by early evening--plenty of time to prepare for a make-or-break meeting.

"I know, the timing is pretty poor for me, too," she said, trying to sound sympathetic, but all she got was a raised brow. "Look, I still know people at the Med Center. If I come with you, we might get more answers than the standard 'the doctor will be in touch,' line they'll give you. I know you don't want to spend more time with me than you have to, but try and put that aside right now. As soon as they collect your marrow, you'll be through with me."

Sandy walked up to their table and slid a smothered breakfast burrito in front of Zac. "I assumed you wanted your usual." She slid an empty plate in front of Jen. "And for you to *just a little taste*, right?"

Zac shook his head. "I haven't stepped foot in the diner in years. How can I be predictable?"

The smell of green chili and cheese wafted around her. Jen grinned. "How about a side of toast?"

Sandy stepped over to the counter and brought back another plate with buttered whole wheat toast. "Didn't know if you really just wanted coffee, or not."

When Sandy left, Zac unrolled the silverware from the white paper napkin with the wildflower imprint in the corner. "Let it go, Jen. I'll go through the tests and donate the marrow. You gave this child up for adoption, she's no longer in your life. So many years have gone by, it's not like we have an attachment to her or anything."

His tone slayed her. "Zac, Carli will always be our child. We made her, we created a human being. I'm sorry I didn't tell you sooner, but there wasn't a good time." She didn't want to get into how abandoned she'd felt. That past was behind her. What she wanted was -- she frowned at the toast before her -- what did she want? Forgiveness? Absolution? "I want you to know I cherish that child because we made her together. I want to be there for her ... and for you."

A strange look crossed his face. He drew a breath as if to say something, then expelled it. Focusing on his plate, Zac shifted in his seat. "I'm sure she appreciates your concern."

He held out his hand. "Let's say grace and eat before it gets cold. We've got a few hours of driving ahead of us."

Jen settled her palm in his and as she listened to the simple thanks Zac offered for their food. He hadn't sent her away.

It wasn't much, but it was a start.

ℂ

"It's highly unusual, but not impossible. Matching the four markers we anticipated, but matching all of them? I'd say that's a miracle." Dr. Prescott frowned as he glanced over the papers in the folder.

"What's your concern, Dr. Prescott?" Jen sat beside him in a matching blue upholstered side chair, her elbows resting on the arms while she tugged at her fingers. "Is there a problem?"

Zac rolled down his sleeves as he glanced around the physician's office, counting the number of diplomas attached to the walls. The man had to have spent most of his life in school. Probably a good thing. The more prepared, the better. From what he'd been through today, he hoped someone knew what they were doing. The tests had taken up pretty much the whole day, most of the time waiting for rooms to open up and technicians stabbing him with needles and questions. With the tests finally behind them, Zac just wanted to salute his opinion of the whole procedure and drive home.

The doctor sat back and tapped his pencil against Zac's chart. Though the staff had been polite to him, Zac thanked the good Lord for the bop upside the head when he was about to tell Jen to hit the road earlier that morning. Like she'd promised, they had talked to a variety of medical staff that, had he come for the tests alone, wouldn't have giving him the time of day.

"For parents to be this closely "matched" with his or her child, both parents must by chance have some HLA genes in common with each other." He glanced from Zac to Jen. "It's very unlikely -- really, we're talking only about a one in a million chance for two unrelated individuals to have the same HLA genes in common -- and then there's only a one in 200 chance that a parent and child will be matched."

"I wouldn't go buying a lottery ticket on those odds." Jen nudged his foot with hers. He looked up as she gave a nod toward the doctor. Zac heard the numbers and had done the math in his head. Tired and hungry, he had little energy for excitement. "So we're a miracle."

The doctor nodded. "As far as matches go, yes. But when we tested the original blood sample, we detected a virus."

"A virus?" That bit of information knocked the tired right out of Zac. Having gotten this far, he hadn't thought a glitch in the road was possible. "What kind of virus? I don't feel sick. "

"It's called Cytomegalovirus, or CMV. It's a common virus." The doctor waved his hand as if considering the amount of information to disclose. "More than half the adults in the United States have it. When people first contract CMV, they develop symptoms similar to a cold, so it's nothing they get alarmed about. The symptoms disappear, but the virus remains hidden in the body."

The muscles across his shoulders tensed. No, this couldn't be happening. They'd come too far. "So, I can't donate?"

"We need to run some tests on Carli. Depending on her status, your virus might actually help build her immunity." He looked over his glasses at Zac. "We'll know more once the results come back."

"So what do we do now?" Jen had moved closer to the desk, the heel of her palm resting on the oak surface. "Can he take something for it?"

"There's nothing more you can do. The virus is something that lives in Zac's body. No harm to him." Dr. Prescott rose from his chair and met Zac's gaze.

"It's all on our end now. We'll check and double check all the results. When we decide whether you're a safe match for her, we'll call you back, and Carli can begin the chemotherapy to prepare her body for the new cells."

Zac pushed back his chair as Jennifer rose and shook the doctor's hand. Prescott offered his hand to Zac. "We will be in touch when we have a better idea of the time frame. I trust the numbers you've given are direct contact numbers?"

He looked at Jen, meeting her relieved gaze with what appeared to be more confidence than he felt. "Connections are sketchy in the mountains. I've given you my direct line, but feel free to contact Jennifer at the ranch if you need to. I know her signals are stronger." A tiny smile lifted the corner of her mouth as she nodded.

"Fine. Stop by the desk and sign the release forms for confidential information." Dr. Prescott shuffled around the desk and clapped Zac on the shoulder. "Many people are registered for donation, but only 1 in approximately 50 actually follow through. Carli is fortunate to have such a close match for her transplant and that your antigen patterns match so closely. Please don't dismiss how rare this is. Without being a sibling, hitting all the markers is truly a miracle. With our experienced team and a lot of prayer, Carli will be a normal little girl again before you know it."

"Good to hear," Zac said quietly as he shrugged on his jacket. He followed Jennifer out the door of the office and into the physician's common waiting area.

"We can get the paperwork over here." Jen tugged on his sleeve as she pointed to the station set up in the middle of the lobby area. "We're almost done."

"Hallelujah." Through all the stress tests, the EKG, the blood drawing, he'd held up like a rock. Frankly, the tests weren't much different than the physical Davidson Enterprises required him to take each year. It wasn't until they sat down in Dr. Prescott's office that the magnitude of what was going to happen slapped him. This was life and death...for another human being...his daughter. He rested his elbow on the counter of the nurses' station while Jen explained what they needed. The stable, foot-wide surface was enough for him to grip and clear away the stars forming around his peripheral vision. Not very heroic to go fainting after the blood-letting was over.

"You okay?" Jen pressed her shoulder against his. "You're looking a bit pale."

The scent of her fruity shampoo competed with the smell of bleached counter tops. "I'm fine. I just want to get going."

As he blinked for vision, he felt her hand slide within his jacket and rub his back. The simple familiar sensation tilted his world back on its axis. How many times in the past had Jen rubbed his back and chased away his anxiety or stress? Too many times to count.

And too disturbing to realize it still worked.

"You need to read this before you sign it." Jen captured his attention as she patted his back before withdrawing her hand. She slipped a sheet of paper in front of him. "I don't want to hear about your secrets without you knowing about it."

"Fine one to talk." He took the release and read every word. The verbiage gave Jennifer the right to his medical history, to be in on major decisions in his life -- on his behalf, if necessary. He scrawled his signature at the bottom, brushing away the thought how strange there wasn't another person he could think of whom he'd give such personal access to his life.

She took the paper and added her signature below his and slid the form back to the nurse. Linking her arm through his, she tugged him toward the glass doors leading to the parking lot. "I could say the same for you. C'mon, we're done here. Let's grab something to eat and go."

⓪

She loved Zac's old truck.

Sitting on the bench seat encased in a saddle-blanket seat cover, Jennifer smoothed her hand over the nubby fabric. Soft to the touch and frayed at the corners, the seat gave the entire cab a homey feeling. She shouldn't have been surprised, Zac Davidson was known for doing some of his best living in his truck. From hunting to fishing to skiing, Zac lived life to the fullest and he used to drag her along kicking and screaming for the ride. Not that she really protested, she smirked to herself. Back then, she would've followed Zac anywhere.

The nostalgia of the truck caught her off guard. Zac made tons of money working for his family. He could've had any vehicle he wanted. Yet he chose to drive the twelve year old Ford truck he'd gotten brand new off the lot for high school graduation rather than trading in for new, two-year leases. She drew a breath, inhaling the ingrained smells of leather chaps, rifle barrel bluing, fleece-lined canvas jackets, and most recently, fast-food sub sandwiches. The touch, the smell, the tastes all evoked memories of that summer, teasing the edges of her mind until she brutally pushed them back. Drawing her splayed fingers into a fist, she sat up straighter and looked out the window onto the darkened highway leading home. Now was not the time to dredge up events that had gotten them here in the first place.

"What's wrong?" Zac gave her the once-over and then returned his attention to the road. "Something spook you?"

Jen rubbed away the goosebumps on her arms. "Just a lot on my mind."

"Yeah, today kicked my butt more than I want to admit."

She let his misinterpretation slide. "I've pulled shifts for years and there were times I didn't think I'd last more than a year or two. The work messed with my emotions so much. The couple of years I worked for my dad at the clinic in Hawk Ridge should have been a vacation for me. Instead, I found I missed the faster pace of working with families and staff. Go figure."

Cars sped past them as the twilight deepened to dark. She tried to concentrate on snippets of the presentation she needed to make tomorrow, but the details played on the edge of her recall.

"You've just got a big heart for folks, Jen."

Her loosely grasped facts and figures scattered. She looked over and caught sight of the firm line of his jaw as headlights from oncoming traffic sped by. She couldn't tell if muscles bunched or if the shadows played with his rugged profile. "It's just what I do."

He met her gaze for a moment, the lines unmistakable beneath his dark lashes, yet the longing in his eyes capturing her heart. They'd had that connection once...a sharing of the mind and soul. A time when she thought she could never live without him.

"It's who you are." He turned his attention back to the road. "Are you sure you had enough to eat? We could've stopped somewhere and ate instead of rushing back home."

The moment -- the connection between them -- vanished so quickly, Jen wondered if she'd imagined it. No, she didn't imagine it. His simple words ignited a yearning within her. One too dangerous to even consider pursuing. Zac not only posed a threat to her prospects of buying the Trails' End, he posed a threat to her overall sanity. Moments ago, she'd blamed her emotional roller coaster on her work at the hospital. Her concern for her patients hadn't held a candle to the puree of emotions he'd left her with.

"I really have to get back. I have a meeting tomorrow and still have prep work to do." That was putting it mildly. All day she'd been mentally categorizing notes on the camp operation. She just hoped she'd be able to pull the supporting data on her presentation before nine o'clock tomorrow morning.

"With the bank? I thought my dad had looked over our figures. Didn't he approve?"

She laughed. Really, didn't the Davidsons ever talk to each other? "He approved. He told me he was going to run the figures by you to see if you approved of them."

"Of course, I do. I put them together."

She released a tired laugh. Why was Zac offended by his dad's concern over her figures? Wasn't he bidding on the property, too? Jen shook her head. Just like always, she hadn't a clue what tree Zac was playing in. "Don't be hard on your dad. He's just happy we looked at the present day layout of the lateral ditches instead of the ones on record." She stared ahead through the windshield. "I have a meeting with the Foundation tomorrow."

"They want a tour of the gorgeous property they're thinking of investing in?"

"No, to review my performance and evaluate my experience." She hesitated going down this road after the day they'd just had. "They're not investing in the property. They're investing in the program. I'm the one buying the ranch."

He sat in silence as the traffic lessened and the highway curved into National Forest. The highway bumped and jostled until they eased over to the passing lane. "So, you could have your camp anywhere?"

Technically, yes. But that option wasn't in her game plan. "No, it's going to be at the Trails' End. That's where I want it."

A few more moments of weighty silence hung between them. "Why?"

"Because that's the way Arthur and I planned it. He knew Jess wanted the money off the land instead of treasuring it for the sake of family inheritance, you know, pass down through the family. Arthur knew I loved the heritage of it as much as he did. The last thing he wanted was the Trails' End parceled off like a tract-home subdivision, which tends to be what developers do these days. Especially with the varied terrain of the ranch. The layout is great for my camp at the plateau just at the base of the mountain rise where we can hike and trail ride, and then I can use the income from the haying operation to help pay, if not pay entirely, the mortgage on the place."

"Sounds like you have it all thought out in a nice, neat package, don't you?" His clipped words hung in the air. "You have no idea how to bring your plans on paper to life in the real world."

"Well, I'm going to have to learn how to manage a camp and acreage sometime, so I might as well learn on terrain I'm familiar with and live on a property with sentimental value."

"Jen," his voice softened. "Take it from me, just because the concept jibes on paper doesn't mean the actual product is going to pan out."

"Well now." She fought to keep her hackles down. "I've just had the greatest minds in Hawk Ridge ranching industry instruct and review my business plan. Are you telling me the Davidson's don't know what they're talking about? Or, did you skew my numbers?"

He released a sigh and stretched his fingers on the steering wheel before wrapping them back in place. "Jennifer, stop it. That's not what I'm saying at all, and you know it. Look at what you're getting yourself into, Jen. It's you and you alone, right now looking at a potential harvest of twenty-four hundred acres. The Circle D can employ a hundred people if we need to, to get the job done." He drew a sharp breath like a calm before the storm. "You've got the right plans...you may not have the power to pull it off."

Didn't he think she'd worried over that? "That's where faith comes in. I never thought I'd get as far as

I have with the camp, much less the bank actually considering my loan application. I'm on my knees every morning and night asking the Lord if this is His will, to help me navigate the trail. So far, I've seen miracles and experienced setbacks. When it's all said and done, all I can say is I tried to listen to His leading."

Oncoming headlights illuminated his hard jaw and set eyes. His lips parted on a puff of breath. "Sometimes in order to follow His leading, you have to let go."

Jen dug her fingers into the saddle blanket fabric. "Zac, I know all about letting go."

"You might know all about it, but are you ready accept the consequences?"

She didn't have the energy left for this kind of mental gymnastics. Zac could talk circles around her when it came to finances and holdings. And he knew it. *Lord, I don't want to argue. Keep my words from evil and my eyes on You.* As she folded her hands on her lap, a sense of peace and calm spread over her, as if God had been waiting for her surrender. She toed off her boots and tucked her feet beneath her on the seat. Shifting around, she settled up against Zac with her head on his shoulder as she'd always done. "I guess I'll find out, won't I?"

Moments passed as they drove along. Without a word, his arm tucked around her, his fingers wandering within the folds of her jacket, pressing her close, just like always. "I guess we will."

« CHAPTER TEN »

MRS. WELLS HADN'T AGED a day in twelve years. Former Sunday School teacher and perpetual president of the Ladies' Aid Guild, she held more love for the Lord in her sterling silver tea spoon than most people could claim in a bushel basket. He'd tumbled in fights with her boys and cheered on her daughters as they barrel raced in high school rodeo competitions. Now the boys ran her ranch and the girls had married, but still lived close to home. Something about small towns just made it tough to stay away.

He stood behind her in the church narthex as she greeted folks coming in the door. Rain or shine, she stood there with a smile making sure folks knew they were welcome. At a lull in the action, he tapped her on the shoulder. "Jon hasn't run you bankrupt yet with his eye on the auctions, has he?"

Her face lit up as she turned around. Grasping his hand in her firm hold, she pulled him into a hug. Years melted away as she patted his shoulder like she had when he was a little boy.

She pulled back and held him at arms' length. "Isaac, nice to see you again. Heard you'd come back for your brother's wedding, but I never saw you."

She waited for his answer with an expectant air. Zac searched for a non-cliché answer. He couldn't find one. "All I can do is beg forgiveness. I'm back for longer now."

"Humph, well, better to see you now than not at all." She shook his hand with a grip to match any rancher. "Don't you go leaving town again without stopping by the house and catching up."

Forgiven. Zac relaxed with instant relief, the kind he didn't even realize he'd been waiting for. The kind he wanted to bask in a while longer. Mrs. Wells had always been his champion, defending his rambunctious behavior to anyone who complained. She'd understood boys, an insight he appreciated to this day. "I'll stop by this week since I'm not planning on leaving."

Her gray eyes studied him before she urged him to go socialize. "Fine. Fine. Come over soon, we'll talk then. My cookie jar is always full. Right now, I have people to invite into the house of God."

He gave her a hug and then turned toward the crowd of people. Folks milled around greeting one another as they'd done for years. A few couples smiled and nodded. A slow warmth grew within him as he greeted friends he hadn't seen in ages. Just like old times.

Funny how some things change and others...just don't.

"Zac. It's been a long time, my friend. Heard you've been harvesting up at the Eklund place." Neal Stricher came up behind him with a cup of coffee in hand.

Zac shook hands and gave Neal a slap on the back. A few years older than Zac, Neal had been a worthy roping opponent. "Word travels, huh? Jess asked me to help out."

"If I'd known that's all it took to get you come back to Hawk Ridge, I'd've asked you to bring in *my* hay a long time ago." Neal cracked a familiar grin. He'd always been built slim; the years of hard ranching had made him solid. "Could've taken Cheryl and the kids on vacation."

Zac laughed. "Didn't think your place was for sale, too."

"Trails' End?" A strange look came over Neal. "I thought Jennifer was buying that for her camp."

"She's got first dibs." He chose his words carefully. "I'm just here to catch crumbs if they fall."

Neal didn't appear to be satisfied. He took a quick sip from his Styrofoam coffee cup and pointed across the room. "She know this?"

Oh yeah. And making the most of every minute of it. He kept his grin in place. "Jen is in a fine position to buy the place, Neal. Like I said, I'm only here for back-up. Besides, I think the camp is great. I've stopped in a time or two." The next words stuck on his tongue. "The camp counselor over there does a great job keeping the kids happy."

Neal's shoulders relaxed. "Glad you and Jennifer talk. When she left to go to school, we didn't think she'd come back either. Glad she did."

"I can't agree with you more." Zac listened for strains of organ music to signal the beginning of the service, but all he heard was Miss Eleanor talking about her summer pies and Jake Small bragging about the high school football team. He turned back to Neal. "Now, what's new in your life?"

Neal went on to chat about his marriage to Cheryl Slaughter, his four kids and expanding cattle operation. Zac listened with half an ear. He found his attention straying to the ride home after his tests at the hospital. What happened there? One minute they were toasting up for a real contest of wills...and the next thing he knew, she was curled up at his side and he'd slung his arm around her. He'd had so much pent up frustration, he wanted to yell. Yet, when he felt her lean close and put her head on his shoulder, he couldn't help but turn on their favorite country station, and kiss the top of her head.

Just thinking about the evening made his insides zing. He nodded at Neal as he scanned the crowd for Jennifer, but came up empty.

Instead, familiar arms wrapped him in a hug. "I'm so glad you joined us for church this morning, honey." His mother gave him a squeeze then stepped back, keeping her hand on his arm. "Is Jennifer here, too?"

"I've only seen Doc O'Reilly." He shook hands with his dad and indicated the back of the room. "Over by the music room."

Martin glanced over Zac's shoulder. "Sure enough. Doc O'Reilly's already nabbed Melanie. Probably scolding her for being on her feet."

Zac peeked over to the group. Doc had a concerned look on his face, Melanie smiled and nodded, Gabe frowned.

And Jen stood beside Melanie, her smile directed at him.

His heart picked up the pace as she broke away from the group and came toward them.

"Grace, Martin. Glad to see you." She stepped up beside him and hooked her arm through his. "There really isn't much room on your family pew with Melanie taking up enough room for a small family." She laughed. "Want to sit with us?"

"Jennifer O'Reilly. Don't go making fun of our Melanie. She's uncomfortable enough as it is." Grace lowered her voice and spoke into his shoulder. "Go on, Zac, sit with Jennifer. Melanie does take up a little more room than usual."

"Not to worry, Mom." He tightened his arm to his side effectively holding Jen's in place. "I want my sister-in-law as comfortable as possible."

Her fingers snagged his sleeve as she tugged him around. "Let's go."

They filed into the sanctuary just as the music rang the final chord. Pastor Dave gave his greeting and the congregation turned to the first hymn of the day.

Zac looked around the sanctuary. Ranchers he'd grown up to respect and admire over the years; pews filled with friends he'd gone to school with who'd remained in Hawk Ridge and started families; a variety of new faces that blended in well with the old. Even sitting in the pew with Jen brought back memories of when they'd attended Sunday services together in high school, sitting at the back of the sanctuary, and holding hands, their sides pressed together from shoulder to knee even though only a couple of other folks occupied the rest of the pew. He remembered holding her hand and marveling over how soft her skin was as the scent of whatever type of light, fruity fragrance she wore teased his nose. He'd had a hard time concentrating on Pastor Dave's message then; right now, he wasn't having an easier time of it.

"Grow up! Act like men!" Pastor Dave stood behind the pulpit, his gaze darting about the men of the congregation. "I know you look like adults - tall, strong, handsome. But age has nothing to do with it. Maturity makes the man, not age."

Zac shifted in his seat as if the pastor had glimpsed his thoughts and discovered Zac's mind elsewhere.

"Let me repeat again what First Corinthians 16:13 says: 'Be on the alert, stand firm in the faith, act like men, be strong.' Of these four commands we're reflecting on today, only "act like a man" is mentioned once in the New Testament. Only once. This is God's wake up call to us, He's drilling His finger in our chests."

His mouth went dry as Zac stiffened. Where had this message come from? Why today of all days? Zac loved the Lord with all his heart, had been a faithful believer since he didn't know when. But no message had ever hit him like this. He glanced around the congregation hoping to see others as taken aback as he. Nothing but calm shone on the faces of the men seated around him. He stole a glance at Jennifer and Doc O'Reilly. They sat still, absorbed in the moment.

"Today's culture is looking for scapegoats-a blame game of epic proportions." Pastor Dave fell silent a moment. "Paul's point isn't any less sharp today as it was two thousand years ago. Isn't it time you take responsibility for your own actions? When you do something wrong, own up to it. Did you cause a problem? Admit it. That's what adults do, they take responsibility for their actions. Behave as men and women. Or better yet, act like ladies and gentlemen. If you give your word, keep it. Maturity. Be faithful and true."

Pastor went on to discuss the last command about being strong, but Zac cut bait on the sermon and stared out the wall of glass behind the altar. A field of wildflowers sloped out of sight with the backdrop of the Elk Mountain Range rising majestically beyond. There was power spoken from the pulpit, but it couldn't match the majesty of the beauty beyond. Zac had given thanks uncountable times for incomparable reminders of God's power and grace in the face of sunlight, storms and darkness. He hadn't remembered giving thought to twilight, but that was obviously the gray area he swam in now.

Be a man. Three simple, straightforward words. Words now burned into his heart. He had a daughter. And as painful as it was to admit, Jen hadn't thought him responsible enough at the time to let him in on the secret. Yes, he'd been hurt when the blood test revealed the truth, but was it his heart that was hurt, or his pride? Or ego?

He bowed his head and studied the crease in his jeans as he sat in the pew of the church where he'd given his heart to God. He and Jen had dedicated themselves to the Lord, along with the rest of their friends during the Youth Gathering when they were in Junior High School. They'd all said the words, and Zac knew deep in his heart, he meant them. How humbling to realize through his self-absorbed strive to succeed he'd let down not only his God, but his best friend and love.

The pastor's words continued to fill the air as Zac clasped Jen's hand and interlaced their fingers. Her muscles jumped, but then she pressed her palm into his and rubbed her fingertip along his knuckle -- just as she used to do. He looked into her trusting blue eyes and saw all the faith she'd ever had in him still glowing. Strands of her blonde hair brushed her cheek as the rest waved over her shoulders. A small grin pulled at his cheek as she stared at him with a curious tilt of her head.

He tugged her closer. "Everything will be alright," he whispered. The same fruity scent teased his nose.

She squeezed his hand. "I know."

@

As soon as Zac opened the door of Leon's Hardware Store, the underlying smell of latex paint, kerosene and spare-parts metal snagged him back to his childhood and Saturday morning shopping at the hardware store with his dad. The old oak floor gleamed with polish, and hanging fluorescent fixtures offered the low buzz of energy that only lamps of that vintage could make. Nothing had changed about Leon's other than an upgraded inventory and state-of-the-art electronics at check out.

His steps echoed as he strolled down the main aisle, new displays of hunting gear catching his eye. A couple of men stood at the counter at the back wall looking at the selection of firearms housed behind locked glass doors. Already the middle of September. Deer and elk season was just around the corner. He needed to check out his own gear before too much longer.

The place had changed just enough for him to search for the machinery parts. He swept past an electronic glass door leading to an outdoor patio. A banner stretched across the doors proclaiming *Garden Center closed until February*. A burst of pride tightened his chest. That was his sister-in-law's doing. When she'd swept into Hawk Ridge two years earlier, she'd not only rearranged his brother's life, but that of the rest of the town. Her bubbly personality had won over the church ladies and her experience with plants and horticulture had won over Elwood Leon. He'd created a position for her giving her a reason to stay in Hawk Ridge; Gabe proposed to her inviting her into the family. Zac didn't know Melanie that well yet, but what he did know, he liked.

"Hey, stranger, what are you doing back in town?" A cute blonde smiled at him as she pointed to his hair. "Looking all rugged and shaggy, no one would believe you've been a city guy for *years*."

Zac grinned at his old friend. "Shayna Leon, you running this store now, or is your dad still the top man?"

"Are you kidding? Dad will always be the top man. And the name is Westin, not Leon. RJ and I got married."

"The cowboy at the Circle D?" Zac remembered reading the name a long time ago. "I thought he was temporary."

"Back then he was. But Gabe liked his work ethics and I liked him. So between the two of us, we convinced him to stay. He partners with Hank doing the stock." She cocked her head. "I thought you knew that? Don't you write the checks?"

"No. Why'd you say that?"

"Because Gabe is always saying you control the money. And you live in Denver. And we never see you." Shayna shrugged her shoulders. "Even Melanie says all the tax stuff and financials need to be run by you."

He managed a lot of the Circle D assets, but writing checks wasn't one of them. "Are you hedging for a raise for RJ?"

"Well, now that you mentioned it," -- she patted her slightly rounded belly, -- "with another baby on the way, some extra money could come in handy."

He laughed as Shayna gave him the thumbs' up sign. "Afraid you'll have to take that up with Gabe and Dad. I've never been part of the hiring or firing or negotiating of compensation. But if you want to start Gabe thinking along those lines, you better start now. The bigger Melanie gets with those twins, the more distracted he becomes. He's going to be a fruitcake by the time the girls make their debut."

"Isn't it great?" Shayna said just as Zac spotted the parts section. He nonchalantly drew her along as she continued to talk. "Melanie is so excited, that's all she talked about this summer. Well, babies and bugs. It's almost spooky how much she knows about spiders."

"She's an entomologist."

"I know, but she's too pretty and nice to get that excited over creepy crawlies." They stopped in front of the order desk for machinery parts. Shayna automatically went behind the counter. "What do you need?"

A big sign behind the desk read Leon's Hardware -- If We Don't Have It; You Don't Need It. Zac grinned at the relic. He'd come into the store when he was just nine or ten and took that sign at its word. He and Jen had plopped a shoe box on the counter in front of Mr. Leon and told him they needed a house for the lizard they'd caught so it wouldn't freeze over the winter. True to the motto, Mr. Leon found an old fish tank in the back of the store, filled it with play sand and taped a heat strip to the bottom of the tank before stacking rocks on it. He even started stocking live crickets in the bait section so Zac and Jen had food for the lizard through the winter.

Jen liked lizards. That had been the coolest thing ever.

He looked down at the part in his hand and shook away the memory. "I had a bolt go out on the baler. Can I hope you have one in stock?"

Shayna took the part. "Give me a few minutes to look for this. We just got a shipment in middle of last week. If Ross has everything inventoried, it won't be hard to find." She turned and disappeared through a door marked "Employees Only."

Zac glanced over the display of rust preventative aerosol cans on the counter and the tower of motor oil stacked behind it. Jugs of anti-freeze lined the shelves along the wall running straight into a display of heavy duty batteries. Pennzoil and Quaker State signs decorated the wall obviously indicating where the motor oil was.

"Zac Davidson?"

Zac turned and found Frannie Pollard standing beside him. "Mrs. Pollard, nice to see you."

"Well, I can certainly say the same for you, young man. I saw you in church this morning, but the Lord frowns on folks discussing business in His house."

"That's what I've always been told and taken to heart." He searched her face for a hint, but all he saw was her studying him. "Are we in business?"

"Oh, not you and me." She stopped glaring and a smug smile dropped into place. She inched closer. "But I do have some interesting news for you."

Thoughts of her three daughters popped into his mind. Frannie Pollard had tried her hardest to get him interested in Peggy when they were in school. Peggy was cute and funny, but never went anywhere without her violin and Zac couldn't hold a tune. They were doomed from the start. "How are the girls?"

"This has nothing to do with the girls. It has to do with the Trails' End Ranch."

A muscle twitched just below his eye. Mrs. Pollard had always had a flair for the dramatic which obviously hadn't dimmed over time. "What about it?"

"You know I work for the title company," she stated as if the position ranked second to the mayor. "And I've been working on the paperwork for Jess Eklund's sale. The secret caught me by surprise...I just found it Friday afternoon. I put a note in my calendar to call Jess, first thing Monday morning." She glanced over her shoulder as if someone was watching them. Satisfied they were alone, she turned back to him and cleared her throat. "Technically - and legally - I should let Jess know about this first, seeing as it's currently his ranch and all, but then you showed up at church today and left so quickly with that nice Jennifer O'Reilly." Mrs. Pollard clicked her tongue as she winked at him. "Saw you sitting with her, too. Nice girl. Hard worker. She's interested in buying this ranch. Did you know?"

"Yes, I'd heard." Dizzy from trying to follow her line of conversation, Zac needed Frannie Pollard back on track. "About the ranch?"

"Like I said, I really should be telling Jess Eklund this first, but you two were always such close friends...and now you're trying to buy the ranch, too...I see no harm in letting you know."

"Mrs. Pollard," he said as evenly as possible. "I wouldn't want you to do or say anything unlawful. I'm just waiting for Shayna to find a bolt --"

As if Frannie hadn't heard him, she clapped her hands together a couple of times and angled her chin toward him. "It's the oddest thing. Everyone in Hawk Ridge knows about the poker game that won ol' Efrain Eklund the Trails' End. That story's been spun around the block for years. Eklunds made a nice place of the ranch, worked it solid and grew good crops. Shame Jess didn't want to stay in Hawk Ridge. But if he hadn't started the process, we wouldn't have ever found out."

The suspense was killing him. "I'm certain Jess knows all about his property."

"I don't think so. No one knew."

His fingers dug into the polished finish of the parts counter. "Knew what?"

"Well, the deed changed hands at the poker game, but Efrain Eklund never did anything with it. He didn't file it, didn't even change names on it."

Sound roared through Zac's ears. He didn't want to guess what she had to say next.

"Isaac, my boy." She drew a breath for dramatics and offered a self-satisfied grin. "The Trails' End still belongs to the Davidsons."

« CHAPTER ELEVEN »

THE AFTERNOON SUN CAUGHT the potted herbs on the kitchen window sill creating long basil and oregano shadows across the oak table. Zac tapped his finger on the wood grain, trying once again to make his father understand. "Dad, the Trails' End belongs to us."

Martin finished digging the meat out of a walnut shell and lifting the last morsel to his lips. Chewing, he raised an unruly brow. "How did you manage to seal the deal before Jennifer's loan approval? What have you done, son?"

"I haven't done anything. And apparently, Efrain Eklund didn't do anything either." Zac stopped short of slamming the heel of his hand on the table top. "The deed is still in the Davidson name."

"My word, Martin." Grace Davidson sat down at the table beside her husband, her gray eyes sharp. "How can this be? We've never paid a cent in taxes on the place." She turned to Zac. "Are you certain Frannie said Davidson?"

Zac nodded, relieved one of his parents grasped the situation. "Yes, ma'am. She made it plain that no one realized the confusion in ownership until she unearthed the title. She did a search on it to see if they'd filed a deed in any other county in Colorado, but nothing came up." He dipped his chin, the words bitter on his tongue. "Looks like you're the proud owners of the entire, original Circle D settlement."

Martin propped his elbows on the table and rested his chin on his hands. "No, I don't, Isaac. You of all people should know what an accounting nightmare incorporating the Trails' End back into the Circle D would be. We'd be digging up records so far back, a few of those years could've been written on scrolls."

"Dad--" Zac began.

His gaze bore into Zac. "You know what I'm getting at. I want none of it. I was perfectly content with the way that gambling story ended and the Eklunds have been good to the place. But you've been on a crusade over that property ever since you heard the tale told 'round the campfire. You romanticized Jeb Davidson gambling the place away, and have been scheming ever since to win the place back." He popped another piece of walnut in his mouth and chewed. "I thank the good Lord every day you turned your brain for numbers in a respectable direction instead of figuring a winning hand with aces high."

Martin sat back in his chair, his expression softening as he took a breath. "I remember you used to pester the daylights out of Arthur Eklund about the history of each building, or an estimate of how many fish were in the stream, or later, how many head of cattle he thought the pastures could sustain. Ol' Arthur had the patience of a saint when it came to all you kids. Jennifer had latched on to him, too. Probably saw him as the grandfather she never remembered. Either way, for the hermit Arthur claimed to be, you'd never know it for the number of kids that traipsed on and off of his land."

"I never assessed the property." Heat tinged the edges of his ears. "I was over there to see Jess."

Shaking his head, Martin chuckled. "You and Jess Eklund and Kade O'Reilly. What a sorry bunch."

"Hey." The conversation was veering off the intended path. Zac tried to steer it back on course. "Dad, Kade and I worked hard. We practiced roping almost every night. We were top ranked on the high school circuit. But that has nothing to do with the Trails' End."

Scratching his grizzled chin, he elbowed his wife. "They're claiming work, Gracie? Is that what it looked like? All that fancy riding and trick roping in the corral with pretty little Jennifer sitting on the top rail cheering you on. I know she clung to Kade like a newborn calf to a heifer after her mom died. But I think she laid claim on more than just her brother's attention."

Zac sat up in his chair and re-crossed his booted feet at the ankles. "She had no choice. Doc O'Reilly worked late. She hung around with us because she had to stay with Kade."

"Uh-huh," Martin agreed. "Until Jess Eklund ripped up the drive on his motorcycle. That boy showed up and all of a sudden you and Kade couldn't cool down horses fast enough." Martin squinted at him. "If memory serves right, you and Kade took off with Jess every time and never took Jen."

Zac looked at his mom, her attention flitting from him to his dad. He didn't really want to discuss this right now. He looked back at his dad and found no quarter. "Jess's plans weren't always...well, they didn't really fit...." Zac ground his teeth over exactly how much to say. Jess had a wild streak a mile long back in the day. "The plans Jess came up with didn't include us taking a girl."

"So, if Jen didn't really need Kade, I wonder why she hung around here?"

Zac stopped in mid-memory. He'd never thought of it that way. Jen never put up a fuss or demanded to come with them. Kade would give her a hug, and then the three of them went to whatever party Jess had caught wind of. Zac never gave a thought to what Jen did after they left. Maybe he should've.

He focused on his folks staring at him and knew he needed out of this conversation. "Dad, the ranch isn't mine."

"If Frannie Pollard says it's still in the hands of the Davidsons, you can take that as truth," Grace proclaimed. "That woman takes pride in what she does and wouldn't have brought it up to you if she wasn't certain. Especially with Jen wanting it so badly for that camp of hers. She and Arthur were awful close."

Wide-eyed, Zac couldn't believe what he was hearing. Desperate to take the focus off himself, he expanded the accountability arc. "What about Gabe? Or Nick? Don't they have a say in what happens to the Circle D?"

"The Circle D, yes. The Trails' End, no. If that ranch is still in the Davidson name, and the taxes are current, the bank doesn't care who paid them. Now, Jess might care, but that's between you and your best friend."

Zac started to rub the back of his neck and stopped. Jess? His best friend? No way.

He'd torn across fields on motorcycles with Jess...but it was Jen's soft laugh tickling his ear as she molded against his back with her arms wrapped around his middle that gave him a full body slam at the moment. They'd ridden a motorcycle together across every hidden path on the Trails' End. Sometimes, they'd be gone all day, her tender nibbling kisses teasing his neck until he'd nearly crashed. Stopping the bike, he'd swept her off the seat to a grassy patch where warm sun and lazy afternoons gave way to him wanting to spend the rest of his life with her.

His eyes grew wide, shocked by the memory. Zac hustled to stuff it back where it belonged. How had such fascinating information gone so far south? Zac had expected an intelligent conversation with his folks over the incorporation of the Trails' End back into the Circle D, not a hot potato toss with a legend that no one wanted to claim.

Clearing his throat, he faced his parents. "If all this is true, what am I supposed to tell Jess? He's planning on using the proceeds to fund an investment he's had his eye on. If that opportunity hadn't come up, he wouldn't be selling the ranch." Zac relaxed as he returned to his original train of thought. "That's all he could talk about when we met and I agreed to cut his hay. He's looking at a deal of a lifetime."

The timer on the kitchen stove dinged, yet Grace stayed seated, the tip of her finger pressed to her lip.

Martin eyed him for a long moment, a lifetime of wisdom milling within his brown eyes. "I don't know, son. I think your worries are misguided. If I were you, I'd be thinking about how to break this news to Jennifer."

©

The activity room of the recreation center was full as Jennifer stepped through the doors. Mentally exhausted after a week of trying to outguess every move Zac made and his motive for making it, Jen looked forward to an evening playing - just her and her kids. She'd spent the final camp session of the season in complete distraction. Digging through buckets of paperwork for the sale of the ranch; Zac Davidson wreaking havoc with her senses; and the biggest weight of all, the little girl she'd borne so many years ago facing life or death...and there was so very little Jen could do about it. She hadn't slept; she hadn't eaten; she felt like a zombie. Thankfully, she didn't scare the children when she smiled at them.

Camp volunteers wove through the crowd, stopping here and there to comment on some accomplishment or newly learned skill. Kids mingled in small groups, girls with girls; boys with boys, all grinning at the attention. Jen smiled. She knew the self-consciousness that went along with cancer recovery. Like a butterfly emerging from its cocoon, the kids had gone through so many transformations during the various phases of chemo and radiation, just grappling with recovery was hard enough.

Throw in adolescent hormones, and the world took on a wilder ride than necessary.

Her heart hurt at the thought of Carli undergoing the same traumatic experience.

"Everyone ready for some fun?" She pasted on a smile and waved her hands. Enough detours off her purpose right now. The kids in the room with her right now deserved her full attention - at least for one night. Getting a thumbs up from Patrick, she glanced toward the kitchen. A small group of girls cheered, but mainly groans from the boys met her enthusiasm.

"Really? Square dancing?" Steven, a lanky boy sporting a new growth of curly, ash blond hair gave her a drawn look. "Are we going to dress in overalls and chew straw shoots, too?"

"I think it sounds like fun," Kelsey piped in, her glasses firmly in place on her nose and sporting the new cowboy boots her parents had bought her right before she came to camp. "Better than video games."

"No way," Brett pointed at the gaming console. "We could play baseball on the Wii. Pick teams. Do all nine innings."

Music started up in the background and a few grown-ups clapped. Patrick came out of the kitchen. "Tonight is our Sunday Night Dance. We've got 22 campers which makes us one pair short."

The remodeled old barn gleamed with new woodwork and lacquered beams. Though she'd had a contractor do the heavy building, she and Tina had worked on some of the finishing touches like painting the window and floor trim, sanding the counter area and polishing the kitchen cabinets. She'd even held the ladder as Tina strung white lights along the rafters. The twinkling lights gave a holiday feel to the barn, no matter the season.

She wanted to turn them on now, but first they needed to calm the chaos.

Patrick began arranging groups, letting the pairs form on their own and only helping the most timid find a partner. Jennifer grinned at the red faces and lop-sided squares. Patrick better have lively music and a quick caller if they were going to keep this group's interest. As she glanced around the room, her attention snagged on the figure at the door leaning against the jamb, his thumbs hooked in the loops of his jeans, a lazy grin on his face. A tingle raced through her as she rubbed her palm down her thigh. The sensation of Zac holding her hand through church still wreaked havoc with her nerves. Would she ever outgrow her embarrassing response to him?

He pushed off from the jamb and walked toward her, the heel of his boots clicking in time to her heartbeat.

"Are we a square of two?" Zac stopped beside her. Warmth emanated through his shirt despite the chilly evening. "I do believe square dancing in gym class was our first hand-holding event."

Jen pushed her hair out of the way and admired how his denim shirt fit his shoulders perfectly. All six-foot of solid Zac Davidson--tall, tanned and toned. What a rush. "I think you have me confused with Laurie Beaumont. I don't think I ever made it to your square."

"Why do I remember it differently? In fourth grade you were my hero," his voice barely above a whisper tickled her ear.

"Because I kept you from flunking out of arithmetic." She matched his whisper and then cleared her throat. "We climbed trees, built forts and had snowball fights. I'm not the one you held hands with."

"Were, too." He reached for her, his hand cupping her shoulder. A shiver followed the path of his touch as he traced down her arm. "In fourth grade, I loved climbing trees and snowball fights. In high school, I developed a fondness for dancing." His finger tip ran along her wrist. "With you."

He took her hand, their palms sliding together perfectly. Her heart pounded as Zac led her across the room to the square with room for two more. He kept holding her hand and stood close to her side. If Jen hadn't held on to her good senses, she could almost believe they were back in school, waiting for the music to start. But her memory painted a wilder picture than the one Zac described. She remembered heated skin and heavenly kisses, with little control between the two of them.

Now that was a memory better off forgotten.

"All right everyone, let's go through the basic steps." Patrick stood in the middle of the three squares, his arms curled at his sides. "To Do-Si-Do, loop your arm through your partner's arm," – he pulled one of the older girls from her partner as he joined Jen's group – "like this, go around each other, then weave your way around the square." The kids stood still as Patrick wove around them. When he got to Jen, he spun her around with a flourish. Caught off-guard, she almost fell over her own big feet. One of the boys snickered. Zac put his hand on her small of her back and steadied her. Heat rushed her face as she reclaimed her place in the square.

Patrick clicked on the music through his remote. "Now try it."

The kids jostled for position. Patrick attempted to be in more than one place at once while other staff members who tried to help just got in the way. Jen angled Zac toward the middle of their square to keep in time with the music, but the kids were so goosey, she stopped and laughed.

Zac snaked his arm through hers and swiveled her and then looped her arm over her head and spun her around as his hand grazed her back. They grabbed hands and pushed back and pulled forward and Zac led her off in a perfect two-step.

"Show off," she chuckled into his neck. "This isn't the dance the kids want to learn either."

"Too bad."

"Eewww. Is that what we have to do?"

Sets of horrified eyes bore into her. The noise level grew and Jen sensed mutiny was on its way. Where was saving grace when you needed it most?

"Don't let any handsome sixth grader steal my spot." Zac squeezed her hand before catching Patrick and pulling him aside.

"Jen, do we have to do this?" A girl pulled her arm from her partner's grip. "Camp is supposed to be fun."

"And well rounded. You keep forgetting that part," she said as she tried to figure out what Zac was up to.

"Can't we save that for school?"

"Attention everyone, we've got a change in plans." Patrick walked over to the kitchen counter and thumbed through the stack of CDs. He pulled one out, showed it to Zac who nodded.

"How about if we forget the Square Dance--"

Cheers filled the room. The boys raced to the flat screen hooked to the video games and flopped down on the furniture. Patrick shook his head and waved them back into place.

"We're going to learn to line dance instead."

« CHAPTER TWELVE »

HE'D INITIALLY COME TALK to Jennifer, to explain about the mix up in ranch ownership. How he'd do his best to help her find the perfect place to move her camp. But when he stepped in the door and saw her laughing with the kids and trying to reassure them they were going to enjoy themselves, he couldn't bring himself to wipe the smile from her face. There'd be plenty of time for her to hate him later. Since church service that morning, he felt his heart shift and it had shifted in the direction of Jennifer O'Reilly. He wasn't sure what exactly he was supposed to do with his rediscovered feelings, but he knew one thing for certain. She needed help and he was the one to give it to her.

Square Dancing. How lame.

But, it was a start.

Zac stepped up and indicated the kids spread out. "This, my friends, is a skill you'll use the rest of your lives." Groans louder than before lifted to the timber rafters as the boys skulked back to their places and the girls inched their way around in one bunch. Zac urged a couple of the girls to the right, the others to the left and shifted the shy to grumpy ratio.

"Lots of western dances start with these easy steps. And we don't have to listen to corny music." He clapped his hands and looked for Patrick. "Patrick? What did you find?"

"Looks like we have just about everything country here." He stood beside the granite counter outside the kitchen. Using both hands, he flipped through a stack of CDs. "What do you want?"

"Brooks and Dunn? Boot Scootin' Boogie?"

Capable fingers snapped up a plastic case. "Got it."

Zac grinned. "All right, campers. Let's have some fun. Form two lines. Go boy-girl-boy-girl." He picked and sorted through the kids as they volleyed for position. Satisfied with his work, he looked around until he spotted Jen.

"Jen, take the back, okay? You've done this as long as I have." He met her bright gaze across the room, her sweet lips parted in a smile that made him want to hang up thoughts of dancing and take his girl out for a moonlight walk.

His girl. Not yet. First he had to tell her he owned the Trails' End.

Shaking away the mood before it ruined his night, Zac looked over the expectant faces filled with a mix of excitement and dread. This was Jen's world now. She had a soft heart, he'd always known that. He'd taken it for granted, too. The Lord had jolted him this morning when He'd grabbed Zac's attention with a swift punch to the conscience, right there between the Gospel lesson and the Offering. He and Jennifer might have a chasm of differences yawning between them, but they also had a thread of common goal that kept them tethered together. Zac was tired of being the outsider in her life. He wanted smack in the middle of the stir.

"See Jennifer O'Reilly, head nurse and chief bandage wrapper back there?" He nodded at her over the herd of adolescents. "Well, she's been known to wear a path in the old wood floor when the right song is playing. And she's partial to Brooks and Dunn, so you guys watch me and Jen will watch you. By the end of the night, you'll be Boot Scootin' all the way back to your cabins."

Girls giggled and boys groaned. Jen stepped back and forth behind the row lining up her crew, a soft rosy glow washing her face. She hugged a little boy who looked uncertain about the whole dance thing and pointed to two of the girls in front of her. She said something to the small group and they all laughed with the boy grabbing the hands of the two girls.

It all appeared so natural, so effortless. Why he hadn't he seen it before? Jen didn't just run a camp. She created a home. A safe place for the kids to be themselves.

And in order for her to do her best at what she did, she didn't need the millstone of a ranch around her neck dragging her down. He'd make her see that first *and then* spring his news on her.

Standing front and center, he waited for the noise to die down. Tonight, he'd help her create an unforgettable night for the kids. He'd help her do what she loved.

"Patrick, you gonna join us?" Jen yelled across the room as she waved to an empty spot beside her. "Zac's one of the best teachers around."

Squaring his shoulders at her praise, he waved to Patrick. "C'mon, Pat. Grab a back seat and let Jen help you along."

Patrick held his hands up. "Someone's gotta run the music. I'll watch and catch up the next time."

"Let's start simple. Watch my feet and follow me." Zac turned his back on the kids. He started with a simple side step, half pivot, foot kick. Rustling and giggles erupted. Glancing over his shoulder, he caught sight of a bit more stepping and kicking going on than called for.

"Whoa there, guys. I can see I need to be a little more hands on." He parted the front line and inserted right in the middle. "All right let's try this again. Side-step, half pivot, front kick. Got it?"

A couple of them got it. They tried again. More got it. Finally Zac waved his arms and pointed to Patrick. "We need music and a demonstration. Jennifer, come up here and help me show our fine audience how it's done."

Her clear laugh called all sorts of memories to mind, but Zac shook them away. He wanted the present. He wanted more. Kids laughed as she picked her way to the front of the room, handing out hugs like salted caramel treats. "Zac's right. Watch how we do it and follow along when you feel like it."

Guitar music filled the room and he began to tap his foot. He'd danced with Jen back when they were in junior high school. Back then, she had to drag him out onto the floor. By the time he figured out girls loved a willing dancer, he decided this dancing stuff was all right. He glanced over at Jen as she moved to the introductory chords.

"Listen to the beat," she was telling the kids. "Start by clapping."

Zac joined in, clapping with her. Soon they began to move and the side step, half pivot, front kick just happened. The kids continued to clap while he and Jen finished one complete move.

"See?" Zac called into the crowd. "It's sorta like square dancing." A little girl at the back of the room twirled around and kicked out an impressive two-step. He waved and caught her attention. "You're a natural. Come up here and help."

She sashayed her way up to the front and stood at Zac's other side. "What's your name, young lady?"

"Kelsey. I love dancing."

"All right, then. Let's do it." With the music blaring, the kids clapping in time, the three of them moving, soon the whole room stepped in time to the tune.

Jen laughed beside him, the sweetest, happiest sound he'd ever heard. "Zac, this is great! They're loving it. You're wonderful."

Warmth spread through him like hot clover honey. Pretty sad situation when such a simple line dance could make him feel ten feet tall. "Ready for a couple more steps?"

The kids cheered. Step-step, hop, kick, turn. Jen danced beside him in fluid motion. Busy watching her move in perfect rhythm, he forgot to turn.

"Zac, the other way." She reached out and snagged him before he tripped over Kelsey.

Her elegant fingers brushed his sleeve sending a zing of awareness straight through him. He caught his step and turned. Kelsey danced on his right, her feet a blur of motion. She clapped and turned and there he was again – a step behind.

"Just checkin' on you." He stepped out of the line before he hurt himself and just watched the fun.

The refrain wound up. "Boot scootin' boogie," the kids all shouted, shaking their hands in the air. Laughter rang along with their cheers of success.

"Way to go." Zac cheered. "You guys just learned your first line dance. You were great."

Jen clapped loud and long for the kids. Golden highlights gleamed as her hair swept across her face in disarray. The tail of her shirt puffed out from the waistband of her jeans. She hadn't spared the energy for the dance that was for sure. His gaze traveled down her long legs to her worn, rust colored boots. He almost laughed. Jen always put fashion in the most utilitarian of terms, her boots not excepting.

"Can we do another one?" Kelsey nudged him from the side. "That was fun."

Zac went into the Electric Slide, using the same steps only adding more. They had a few dancers slip and slide through the steps, but everyone caught on to the rhythm and even got their turn rights and turn lefts. By the end of the evening, he looked across a floor full of happy, tired faces.

Patrick punched off the music. "So are you telling me this was more fun than square dancing?"

An automatic cheer went up. Patrick shook his head. "Guess I better spend my winter brushing up on line dancing for the next season of campers, unless you want to stick around, Zac?"

His heart jumped to this throat. He planned to stick around. He wasn't so certain about the camp. "It's a great place."

"I know. Isn't it?" Jen brushed up against his arm and gave him a hug. Without thinking he encircled her waist and drew her closer, the soft tone of her laugh echoing into his chest. He felt like a heel the whole time he held her, knowing by the end of the week their relationship would never be the same again. God help him, he didn't want to think that far ahead. He hadn't a clue of how this whole thing could possibly turn out well.

"This is it, Zac." Jen caught her breath. "This is what the Trails' End is all about. Letting go and being yourself. God's grace and mercy at its best. They had a blast."

He breathed in the scent of her warm skin as he rubbed his nose in her hair. "So did I."

"Me, too." Jen swayed in his grasp. "You can do everything, Zac."

He shook his head. "I'm just an old cowboy, good at training horses, cutting hay, and taking a turn around a dance floor. Nothing special about that."

Jen's arms tightened around him. Her green gaze soft and promising. "You've always been special, Zac Davidson. And if you weren't so full of yourself, you'd see it."

If they didn't get out of the barn right now, he'd show Jen and everyone else there how full of love he was for Jennifer O'Reilly. Stuffing his arms in his jacket, he clasped her hand and tugged her toward the door. "C'mon. It looks like your folks have everything taken care of."

§

Jen hesitated as Zac tugged her toward the door, his warm fingers tangled in hers. Patrick and a couple of the house parents were gathering the chairs and sweeping the floor. Tina stood beside the stereo speakers, grinning at her. When she opened her mouth, Tina frowned and waved her away before catching Patrick and handing him a stack of electronics cords.

She bumped into Zac's shoulder. He pressed close, his arm settling around her waist. "Are you okay?"

She'd been dismissed by Tina which was better than asking permission to leave. "Of course. I just had a great night of dancing and the kids are all happy about it. Life couldn't be better."

"Doesn't take much to make you happy, does it?" He held the door open as they stepped out into the cool night air.

Jen waved to the campers as they ran around under the glow of the yard lights. She spotted a couple of counselors standing along the corral fence watching the kids and Jen relaxed. "It never has."

"Oh, I don't know. I remember a gal all bent on getting into the right school years ago. Had to have a good pre-med program. Had to be DU. You can't tell me your little world wouldn't have caved if the University of Denver hadn't accepted you."

She rubbed her face against the hoodie jacket he wore, releasing the scent of Old Spice and taking her back years. "Getting that scholarship was sweet. Made my dad happy, too."

"I was proud of you." He hugged her close as they followed the trail to her house. "Academic, full-ride. Everything you'd always wanted."

He grew quiet. Jen basked in his praise. "I was proud of you, too. Rodeo, full-ride. I'll never understand how you coupled team roping and math."

"The same way I did it all through high school, a little luck and a whole lot of praying." Their steps crunched along the dirt path in time. "It wasn't just me, remember? If you hadn't tutored me when I had pneumonia, I probably never would have understood the way numbers worked together."

She leaned into him as she kept time with his stride. "What else was I supposed to do? Your family took us in when my mom died, and then you had to go and get sick. I was just trying to keep you from driving your mom nuts."

"You and Kade could've ignored me and watched TV."

"Yeah, I guess we could have, but then Kade wouldn't have figured out you knew your way around the end of the steer he couldn't quite figure out."

"See? Hooking up with Kade for team roping got me the rodeo scholarship, and hooking up with you to help me with my math homework flicked the *I got it* switch in my brain." He hugged her closer. "I came up with the hooking-up-with-you-as-my-girlfriend all by myself."

Her throat burned at his tone of longing. High school had been a great time. Too bad all good things came to an end. She laughed with half a heart. "I made you sit down and study, and you made me close the books and have some fun."

"Guess we were quite a pair." They slowed as the yard light behind her house shone through the trees in the distance. There were times she thought the distance from her house to the barn was too far...tonight, it wasn't far enough. "Probably a good thing we didn't go to the same college after high school. We wouldn't have gotten any studying done. Or at least, I know I wouldn't have gotten any studying done."

A fleeting image of his dorm came to mind, but she pushed it away. Not tonight. All she wanted was one good night with Zac. "God knew what He was doing, no matter how much I pouted."

They got to her porch, the light of the crescent moon behind the towering pine almost picturesque. Zac loosened his hold of her, but didn't let go. Jen turned in his arm so she could see his face, relish the moment. His brown eyes blended with the shadows making it impossible to read his thoughts, but shifted in all the right places making him look like cowboy legend. Zac had always been larger than life to her. Even now, her heart thumped in her chest just like it used to whenever she saw him.

"I'm sorry you pouted." He drew her closer until his breath warmed her cheek. "I would've fixed that."

Her heart pounded as he swept along her cheek, his shallow breathing warming her skin from her ear to the corner of her mouth. She waited for him to pull back, but instantly realized that wasn't how she wanted the evening to end. "Zac," she mouthed against the rasp of evening stubble on his chin. Turning the slight degree between yes and no, she captured his lips with her sigh.

As if time had never passed, her arms slid into place around his waist, her fingers tangling in the folds of his shirt. The solid muscles of his back moved beneath her fingers as she pressed her palms and absorbed the warmth of his smooth skin. His hands slid along her curves before his arms wrapped around her, his hands kneading her shoulders, the heat from his fingers scorching through her shirt. His lips coaxed and teased, and Jen trembled at the effort to contain her need. Zac drew back as if realizing her struggle. The depths of his dark eyes told her all she wanted to know. He reclaimed her lips and she surrendered to the faint taste of peppermint and deepening passion.

Through the blur of her desire, she became aware of his phone ringing in his back pocket. Jen ran her fingers across the denim, trying to silence the disturbance. Zac's hand stroked her fingers as he pulled the phone out of this pocket. Breaking away, he looked at the screen and frowned. In the inky darkness of a mountain night, the bright screen illuminated like a flashlight in a closet.

"Davidson." He held the phone to his ear, his head bowed until his forehead touched her head, fighting for control of his breathing. Jen savored the effect and linked her fingers as her arms encircled his waist.

"Yes, that's sounds good." Zac nodded his head though the caller couldn't see. "Got it. I'll be there." He clicked off the phone.

Zac gathered her up and held her close, resting his chin atop her head. Feelings of happily ever after ran like warm syrup through her veins. She'd missed Zac. She'd missed him so much. *I lost him once, Lord. I don't want to lose him again.*

"Zac--" He kissed her again before she could finish her sentence. A kiss that spoke of need and desperation. A kiss that she matched breath for breath. When he broke away again, Jen growled in frustration. "What?"

"They can use me. They want my bone marrow."

Shaking away the silken threads of their kiss, she frowned. "They called? Now? Tonight?"

He drew her to him until not an inch of space separated them. "It was your friend from the lab. He said he tried to call you. When you didn't answer, he called me."

"Zac, it's Sunday night." Her heart beat at a tempo to match his. She rubbed her nose in the cotton trim of his jacket and drew a deep breath of warm, male scent. When Zac didn't speak, her mind began to create scenarios. "What's up?"

His lips trailed light kisses through her hair. Her lids fluttered closed as she pressed her ear to his chest, calmed by the strong thud of his heart beat.

"They have an opening Friday at the hospital in Denver. He wanted to book it with consent." He squeezed her tighter. "I'm thinking of our daughter."

Our daughter. Jen buried her face in his jacket so he wouldn't see the tears she couldn't hold back.

« CHAPTER THIRTEEN »

STEAKS SEARING ON THE GRILL.

Zac inhaled the mouth-watering scent even as he imagined the flames licking around the tender cut of rib-eye steak with his name on it. Charred on the outside; rare in the middle. No one served steak better than Fred's Grill and Watering Hole. He'd been to the finest restaurants in the country and nothing compared to the food and atmosphere at Fred's.

A lady bumped into him as he directed Jennifer past a cluster of teenagers and a couple each dressed in leather from head to toe. A tiny spot opened up in the corner of the waiting area beneath the mount of a trophy bass. They slid into the space just at the massive oak doors opened up again and another group of four entered the foyer.

"How long a wait?" Jen squeezed into the crook of his arm as the couple in leather followed in their wake and leaned against the wall next to them.

"About fifteen minutes. They're due for a change of diners anytime now." He wrapped his arm around her and pulled back giving him access to her dainty ear. "Maybe I should have slipped him a twenty to get us moved to the front of the line."

She snuggled closer. "We'd have a mutiny on our hands."

"No thanks, I just got out of one."

She lifted her head from his chest, her hair tickling his nose. "Don't kid yourself. This is more like a temporary truce. If you're shelling out for a dinner at Fred's, I thought I'd better be nice to you."

"You're doing just fine." Her face flushed at his conspiratorial wink. He kissed the tip of her nose. "Not even prime rib from Fred's compares to kissing you."

"Mmm, let's not be too hasty." Her grin let him know she felt the same. "Let me think about this."

Running his hand down her back, he splayed his fingers across her ribs, testing her toned muscles. "Don't forget I'm putting my life on the line day after tomorrow."

"You'll be asleep. You won't feel a thing."

The thick murmur of her voice set his blood racing as he nuzzled her ear. "How do you know?"

"Because I'm going to be there and make sure nothing happens."

Zac stopped his quest and straightened. "You're coming with me? I thought this was supposed to be a secret. How are you going to explain going to Denver with me and leaving your camp on the last weekend?"

Another set of diners walked through the doors. Couples shifted and Zac pulled her deeper into the corner. Jen looked across the entry and then back at him. "Don't worry about how I handle the camp. I have it all in hand. Besides, the extraction of your marrow is a day surgery. They check you in first thing in the morning, prep, knock you out, wake you up, and send you on your way. You'll be a little sore, but nothing like what Carli will have to go through. Besides," she paused and ran her finger along his jaw. "How do you plan to get back home? You won't be able to drive."

He kissed the tip of her finger. "Friends."

Her body tensed and she dropped her hand. "Friends. Of course."

What had he said? "You make that sound like a crime."

"No. No, it's not. It's just a statement of fact." She tried to squirm out of his arms. "You're a pied piper of people. You'll never be alone."

He held tight. "Is there anything wrong with that?"

Her shoulders drooped and she stopped pushing him away. "I'm just going to the hospital to make sure everything goes alright with the marrow extraction. If you want me to drop you off at a friend's house, just give me the address."

"Look, Jen, I'm not trying to start a fight here." He gathered her close until she relaxed and molded to his side again. "You're the one who said you were coming with me. I thought end of camp weekend was a big thing. I didn't want to take you away from anything important."

"I guess I'm a bit more nervous over this procedure than I thought." She searched his gaze, the crystal blue of her eyes but a thin ribbon around her pupil. "I shouldn't have assumed you even wanted me there."

Returning her intense gaze, he realized the depth of her concern. "Nothing would make me happier than knowing I had company to keep me awake on my way to the hospital. Someone to hold my hand when they wheel me off. Someone to be holding my hand when I wake up."

"Someone?"

"You."

Her brilliant smile lit her face and he remembered why he'd fallen in love with her all over again.

The hostess called his name to be seated before he could devour her without a thought to being in public. At a back table, the noise level from the crowd dropped letting the soft flow of easy rock music lull the patrons. Candles housed in low lanterns in the center of each table created an atmosphere of endless possibilities. All Zac wanted was a relaxed evening where he might explain the situation of the ranch to Jen and if he were lucky, maybe even get a good night kiss out of her.

"Hey guys, been a long time since I've seen you two out together." A waitress stopped beside them and nudged Zac.

"Hey, Picone," Zac greeted the former high school rodeo queen and four time chess champion. "Great to see you again. Didn't think you were still around."

"It's not Picone anymore, it's Monacelli." She flashed her wedding ring. "Shelly Monacelli. Don't laugh, a gal can't help who she falls in love with."

"No way am I ever going to laugh at the gal who fed me my lunch every time we played chess." He nodded toward Shelly. "You ever play her? Talk about a mind that mapped out the entire chess board before I ever made a move. I still bow to the master."

"Nope, not a chess kinda gal. I spent my time helping her fluff her hair and polishing the hooves of her horse." Jen pointed her thumb to her chest. "That finished product you saw galloping across the arena? Thank me."

Shelly laughed. "Oh, back in the day, right, Jen? Zac, I haven't seen you in ages. Home for a visit?"

He felt Jen's eyes on him. "Cutting hay at the Eklund place."

"Jen's ranch?" Shelly beamed. "I knew you two would always get together again. I just never dreamed you'd be the hired hand on Jen's place. What a wacky world."

"Shel." Jen fingered the menu on the table before her. "Zac is working for Jess, not me."

The reminder of things left unsaid turned his tongue to sandpaper. He coughed and reached for his glass of water. He didn't relish telling Jess about the Trails' End deed, but the thought of telling Jennifer punched his heart. "Last time I looked, the Circle D signed my paychecks, but hey, I'm open to all offers."

"Doesn't matter, does it?" Shelly looked back and forth between them. "He's back, you're back. I'd say that's a pretty good start to happily ever after."

Jen cleared her throat and made a show of opening her menu. "What's the special tonight?"

Shelly rattled off the specials and made her recommendations. Jen placed her order, as did Zac.

"Zac, the rib-eye; Jen, the filet. Both burned, but pink." She smiled as she folded her hands without writing anything on her pad. "I could've almost called it. I'll get this right out."

Watching Shelly walk away, Jen frowned. "Are we really that predictable? Funny, I guess my tastes haven't changed."

He reached over and linked his fingers with hers. "I'm glad. Gives me hope."

"Hope for what?"

"That maybe there's hope for second chances."

She blushed. "You're still the charmer."

"I'm serious."

"You get whatever you want. You don't need to add me to your list." Her gaze softened. "Zac, I know I've hit you with some pretty big issues over the past couple of weeks. Things I know you never expected to hear. Thank you for everything."

He didn't want her appreciation. He wanted her heart. "What happened to us, Jen? You were miserable over us leaving for different colleges, then I couldn't get a hold of you no matter how hard I tried." He shook his head and laughed. "I saw enough of your roommate to make folks think I was going out with her."

"I'm sorry I missed you." She looked down at the table, the corners of her mouth tight.

"Why didn't you return my calls?"

Her fingertips pressed into his hand as she continued to stare down.

He swallowed to moisten his dry throat. Rubbing the side of her finger with his thumb, he tugged at her hand until she looked up. "I would've been there for you, you know. You didn't have to go through the pregnancy by yourself. Why didn't you talk to me?"

"Because," she said as she blinked the tears from her eyes. "You had moved on."

"What are you talking about?" Frustration over her evasiveness during the past week swelled in his chest. "I hadn't moved anywhere other than from the Circle D to the dorm. I had classes up to my eyeballs. I didn't have time to move anywhere."

She tried to untangle her fingers from his, but he held firm. He wanted to know why she'd kept this from him and he was going to get it. "Jen, tell me."

She sat there, her gaze riveted to the napkin in her other hand. Lips pressed together, she silently worked through her answer. Closing her eyes, her dark lashes fanned across her cheek as the muscles in her delicate jaw pulled and eased. Finally, she tilted her chin and opened her eyes, meeting his gaze square on. "I did come to tell you. A week after I found out I was pregnant. I drove to your dorm and asked to see you."

"When? No one told me."

"I can understand why."

@

Jen tried to yank her hand free again, but Zac held firm. His brown gaze sharpened and all the stubbornness she'd ever known Zac to possess came to a head. He wasn't going to let this drop. Muscles clenched until her stomach hurt. She knew she'd have to tell him sometime.

She just hadn't thought that sometime would be tonight.

Swallowing, she forced her voice calm, her words slow. "When I realized I was pregnant, my brain sort of imploded. I'd made plans...you'd made plans...we were both finally out on our own and working on our futures." Acid built up in her stomach, but she couldn't stop. She had to tell him the truth whether he wanted to hear it or not. "A month into classes and I find out it wasn't my cooking making me sick. You have no idea how I struggled trying to figure out a way to deal with this so no one hated me."

"Hated you?" The pressure of his squeezing her fingers eased, but he continued to hold her. "I could never hate you. Why would you think that?"

Years of repressed insecurity shot to the apex of her brain. When her mother died, Jen's world collapsed. She'd expected her dad to wrap her in a hug and assure her everything was alright, but instead, he avoided her and buried himself in work, staying away from the house as much as possible. She'd clung to Kade, but he had better things to do with Zac and Jess Eklund. When her dad had dropped them off at the Circle D, she'd felt abandoned and displaced. Grace Davidson had done her best to comfort the confused girl thrust into her care, but even Grace had little time to reassure her, to convince Jen that she'd never go away.

She'd been a burden to everyone.

The chatter of guests seated around them brought her back to the restaurant and Zac. He let go of her wrist and leaned across the table, his muscled arms and broad shoulders attesting to the man he'd become. A man who spent his days cutting hay for his best friend and his nights keeping books for the family business. And still making time to help her with problems way beyond her control. Gazing into the deep, dark brown eyes that expressed every emotion churning within him, Jen could almost believe he'd never hate her.

Almost.

"I'd tried calling your room the week before, but I never caught you or your roommate, and dorm phones didn't have voice mail. So after classes on Friday, I drove up to your dorm hoping I could catch you. The lobby was crowded with kids clumped together in groups talking or playing pool. I asked the front desk to ring your room. The guy said he'd just seen you playing pinball." She stopped, not certain how to proceed. Zac's shoulders had tensed and she sensed he anticipated the next part. "I found the pinball machine...and you..."

His hand fisted. "And?"

"You weren't alone, Zac." The bitter taste of the words spread through her mouth. "And when you won the game and grabbed her and kissed her, I figured she wasn't some casual observer."

He sat silent as people walked past their table and flatware clanked on plates all around them.

"You'd moved on. This was what you'd always dreamed of...it was all you ever talked about. I wasn't going to be burden." Her throat constricted until she could barely breath.

"I'm not going to lie, Jen." He unfisted his hands and locked his fingers together. "I went wild my first semester at Colorado State. I loved living in the dorm, meeting people...party-ing."

Nodding her head, she refused to look at him. Zac had always attracted people and made friends easily. What girl in her right mind wouldn't have wanted Zac Davidson's attention?

"And, nearly flunked out." His ragged breath made her look up. "I looked for focus, the problem was, I focused on everything that didn't involve studying. When I came home for Christmas break, I couldn't wait to see you, to find my footing again."

She blinked. "To use me."

"No, to tell you the grass wasn't any greener on the other side of the mountain range. I needed you to ground me and you didn't come home."

She squeezed her eyes shut, unable to look at Zac. He'd needed her to help him find his way? Oh what a pair of mixed up teenagers they'd been. The last thing she'd wanted was the censure of the people she'd loved and respected...her father, the Davidsons...and Zac. That night, she ran from his dorm, and once home, she'd dropped to her knees and begged forgiveness from a loving God. For mercy and grace.

And a way to cope with her inconvenient pregnancy.

Memories of that Christmas came flooding back. She'd sought refuge with her roommate and her family. The love and acceptance poured over her by the large family had brought peace to Jen's soul. That Christmas Eve, as they sat in the family pew listening to the story of the lowly birth of the King of Kings, Jen released her possessive hold on her unborn child and ask Jesus to give her child the life she deserved. Feeling Jesus in her heart kept her from going insane.

"Jen." Zac's ragged voice brought her back from her reverie. He ran his hand through his hair. "I can imagine how bad that looked, but it's not what it looked like."

She couldn't make a sound. Her heart pounded so hard in her chest, she thought she was going to pass out.

"I'll admit, I went wild that first semester. I'm not proud of it." He held his palms open to her as if offering a sacrifice. "That's all it took for you to lose faith in me?"

The bleak look on his face tore her apart. "It was November and I was a hormone milkshake trying to keep it together studying, worrying, and trying to cope with my changing body."

"I stopped by your apartment in Denver a couple of times when I was in town. Your roommate didn't say anything to me about you being pregnant."

"I asked her not to." She looked at him. "But the naked truth hit me in the face--I was eighteen years old and having a baby."

White edged his lips as his jaw worked. "*We* were eighteen and having a baby."

Her last vestige of pride broke loose at his plea. "Since you never told me you loved me, I figured I was one of the memories you took with you, a stepping stone, so to speak." She drew a breath. "I know how much you valued your freedom."

"I can't believe this." A choked laugh punctuated his incredulous tone. "You gave away our baby because you thought I'd resent it?"

She stopped a moment, the heat of their conversation stirring the air between them. She wanted to reach out and touch him, though touching him was the last thing she should do. "Zac, every child is a gift from God. A gift that deserves all the love and care she can get. At the time, *we* wouldn't have been able to do that for her. But another family could." She sniffed, drained of emotion, Jen couldn't give any more. "You couldn't get out of Hawk Ridge fast enough to start your new life."

The muscles in his forearms worked as he fisted his hands. With obvious control, he pounded them together and leveled his dark eyes until she couldn't have looked away if she wanted to. "I left Hawk Ridge because of you."

« CHAPTER FOURTEEN »

HER EYES GREW WIDE as all color drained from her face. She moved her lips, but no words came out until she drew a breath through flared nostrils and folded her hands on the table. "You left because of *me*? *I* made you leave Hawk Ridge? I handed you my heart and soul, and...and...innocence, and you...you...."

With jerky movements, Jen pushed back her chair and rose from the table. Grabbing her purse, she dodged her way through the crowd.

Zac sat with his mouth open. That had definitely come out all wrong. Rising from his chair, he had to stop as the hostess showed a family to their table. He curved around the little boy dawdling behind the others and scoured the waiting area for Jen. Where had she gone? He swallowed the desire to cuss up a storm. The evening had started out so right, how had it gone so wrong?

Unwilling to stand guard over the ladies' room door, Zac pushed through the massive oak doors into the cool evening air. The scent of grilling beef filled the air as more couples strolled the sidewalk to the entrance. Had she stayed inside? He prayed not. The thought of drilling back and talking to Jen with people pressed all around hurt his brain. He skirted a couple of low bushes and crossed the lawn to the wrought-iron gate that enclosed the small patio. Soft laughter and talk filtered through the hedges camouflaging the gate and fences. He checked up and down the street. Cold fear built in his chest. What if she'd managed to lose him in such a short time? If Jen wanted to remain hidden, she knew how to do it. Twelve years ago, she'd disappeared from his life and he never caught a glimpse of her.

A movement down the street caught his eye. He'd recognize that sweater and slim-fitting jeans anywhere. Forcing himself to approach slowly, Zac kept his gaze trained on her as she leaned against the brick planter filled with late summer marigolds down at the end of the block. Emotions collided in his brain and crumbled to his heart as he watched her shoulders quiver. He wanted to turn and walk away, abandon her like she'd abandoned him. But even as the thought flitted in his mind, he shook it off. There were no right or wrong answers, only a past they couldn't change.

He stepped closer and folded her within his embrace. Her arms slipped loosely around his waist as she buried her face in his chest and cried until her tears soaked through his shirt. He stroked her hair, his fingers tangling in the thick strands much like the evening they'd shared before he'd left for school twelve years earlier.

The night that changed their lives.

He ran his fingers through her hair until he cupped her scalp in his palm. "Shhh, Jen. You made the right decision. As much as my pride is shouting that I've been wronged, my conscience tells me I did you wrong. I'm sorry, Jen."

As her crying grew still, she ran her finger along his leather belt until she hooked onto a belt loop. Holding her felt right, like she'd been made for him. Just like always.

Giving her a squeeze, Zac busted the last of his pride to dust. "Jen, I didn't leave because I wanted to. I left because I knew if I didn't leave soon, I never would. I had to see what I was made of." He ran his hands down her shoulders and held her still. "You claim I never told you I loved you." He kissed the top of her head. "Let me tell you now."

Tracing the tip of his finger along her collarbone, he followed the soft skin and tilted her chin until her watery, blue eyes shone in the faint light of the street lamp. The pulse in her throat quickened. She was the only one for him, she'd always been. He lowered his head and claimed her soft lips. A low moan escaped her as she returned his kiss with a passion to match his own. Her eagerness for his touch messed with his equilibrium. They'd been made for each other.

Zac pulled back, his heart pounded in his chest. "Jen, I love you."

She gazed up at him, the truth of her love in her eyes. "I never stopped loving you."

His conscience nudged him to put some space between them, to push back emotions until they discussed the transplant, the adoption, and especially the ranch, but she felt so good in his arms and looked at him with such trust in her eyes, he decided to hold his cards close to his chest for a little longer before playing his hand. He'd just reclaimed what he thought lost to him so long ago. Uncertainty colored the days ahead and Zac wanted to bask in the reality of the present as long as he could.

"I love you, Jen. I should have told you long ago, but I knew I had to break away from the Davidson name -- do it all myself -- and make it through school, make it on my own. You've always been my friend, but you've been my crutch, too. I learned the importance of self-motivation and discipline from you, but I had to see if I could hold myself to the line." He grazed the pads of his thumbs beneath her eyes, reveling in the softness of her skin. "I thought I had done so much and come so far, only to find out you still run laps around me when it comes to responsibility."

"You did what you had to do and I faced the obstacles that were put in front of me." She sniffed and rubbed her nose. "I know our lives would be different if we'd kept the baby and I guess we'll never know if it would've been better or worse. All I care about is that God brought us together again now." She squeezed him tight. "I've missed you, Zac. So many times over the years I wished I could've called to ask your advice or opinion on something. Or just to talk. You were always my best friend."

He smiled. "Yep, Bean. We were definitely two of a kind."

She laughed. "Quit calling me that. I've filled out."

"You most certainly have. And I love the new and improved Bean just as much."

She hugged him. "I'm glad you're here."

He bent and captured her lips again, her sigh enough to let him know she felt the same. Her summery scent drifted around him. So many memories seeped back, he couldn't keep it all straight.

She broke the kiss and searched his face. "Zac? Are you scared?"

His conscience nipped at him again. He'd scoured the social site for every bit of information he could glean about Carli Seacrest. He saw love in a family that God had pieced together - all the Seacrest children had been adopted - and accepted the fact everyday life was good for his daughter. He felt a bit uncertain about the transplant - having never been one to relish the unknown, but still, the outcome of the procedure didn't scare him as much as telling Jen she wouldn't be buying the Trails' End. He couldn't bring up the ranch now. He'd find a way to tell her after the procedure. When they could give the matter their full attention.

He tightened his embrace. "Only that you might leave me again," he whispered in her hair.

She pressed her fingers along his ribs as if counting them, her palms pressing him closer to her. "I couldn't leave you if I tried."

❦

Cheers floated in through the open health room window. Jen grinned knowing the kids were having fun as she stared at the stack of papers scattered around her. Maybe she wasn't cut out to be a paper pusher. Health forms and reports vied for her attention, the monotony of legalese and standard issue directives from the hospital board a counterbalance to her whirling emotions. She wanted to get it all done so she could spend the day with Zac tomorrow and not feel guilty about leaving her work undone.

The echo of another whoop floated into the office. "Sounds like the kids are having way too much fun. I don't see a ballgame going on. What are they doing?"

Tina Fenwood looked up from the box of meds she was inventorying. "Last time I looked, there was a crowd along the corral fence. Maybe Patrick has some sort of jousting competition going on."

"Hmm." Unscheduled activities caused alarms to go off in Jen's brain. She backed from her desk, uncertain she wanted to discover the source of excitement. "I'm sure it's nothing."

Stepping out of the health office, an errant breeze bathed her in pine scent. Another cheer went up as she turned and headed toward the corral. Even from a distance she could tell Patrick had nothing to do with this excitement.

Zac sat atop a sorrel horse, both horse and rider focused on a group of steers across the corral. His lips moved and the horse turned to the left. Up a few paces and quick reflex action, the pair skillfully cut a bald-faced steer from the herd. The steer angled back only to have the horse sidestep in the way. Zac held the reins yet allowed the horse to work the prize to the back corner of the pen before pivoting around and setting the steer free.

The campers loved it. Zac grinned like a kid who'd scored a grand slam for the home team. The horse looked pretty proud, too.

Zac urged the horse to the fence and caught her eye across the compound, his triumphant smile giving a crooked tilt to his lips.

That was all it took? One look from the back of his horse, one guileless grin, and her heart melted like winter ice on the Gunnison River in spring thaw. She couldn't begin to wonder how she'd avoided seeing him all these years.

"Alright, everyone. Show's over. Thanks for being a great audience." Zac urged the horse to the gate. "I've got work to do before the boss lady fires me."

She looked up as heat bathed her neck. "I'm not the boss lady, and you're not the entertainment. Last time I looked, that was Patrick's job."

"Are you going to work with him tomorrow?" A tall, thin boy with glasses stood on the bottom rail of the fence panel, arm stretched out to pet the horse. "This is cool."

"Not tomorrow, Brett, I've got something going on." Zac winked at Jen. "But if all goes well, I'll be back Saturday to see you guys before you leave."

Always the optimist, Jen had to give him credit. They'd said harvesting the cells was day surgery, but that didn't mean Zac would be ready to party with his new BFFs. "Okay everyone, snack time in the barn. Mr. Zac needs to get back to work."

"See?" Zac winked at Brett. "Boss lady."

Brett giggled and ran off after his friends.

"Why are you commandeering the kids? Patrick has the schedule all worked out."

"And who do you think gave me permission to entertain the troops?" Lifting his leg over the saddle, Zac hit the ground with grace, his denim jeans molding over his long legs like a second skin. Reins in hand, he stepped over to the fence, his cowboy walk better than any swagger.

Heat raced up her neck. Fine thoughts to be having just before surgery. "Didn't the doctors tell you to take it easy or something today?"

Tipping his cowboy hat back, he grinned causing the dimples she loved to run deep. "I had to prove I was a cowboy."

She cleared her throat. "Why? I told them you're a cowboy."

"Goes with the mystique of the ranch." He indicated his body with a sweep of his fingers. "Riding jeans, western shirt, cowboy hat. Gotta look the part. What self-respecting cowboy wears ball caps and hiking boots? Besides, Shiner here hasn't been worked much. I thought I'd give him run."

The smell of sweat and dirt woven with the scent of healthy male drifted over her. She closed her eyes and took a deep breath--for composure. She didn't want to get drawn into his twisted logic. She just wanted to get surgery over with and figure life out from there. Opening her eyes, she leaned against the fence and look into his sweaty, grimy, handsome face. "You are too much."

He leaned closer until the brim of his hat bumped her forehead. His strong jaw tempted her until she couldn't help but run her fingertip along the smooth skin, stopping as his shaggy hair curled over his ear. "You need a haircut, cowboy."

Peppermint scented breath warmed her cheek. "I think I need more than a haircut."

Firm, gentle lips captured hers. Jen didn't care she stood in the open, beside a corral, in broad daylight. She kissed him back with a hunger that belied her earlier words of caution and taking it easy. There was nothing easy about her feelings for Zac Davidson. If anything, they confused her more than anything she'd encountered her entire life.

The scuff of reins hitting the ground came moments before his palm cupped her jaw and Zac deepened their kiss. Jen looped her arms around his neck and pressed against the corral fence that separated them. A low growl rose in Zac's throat as he snaked his arm through the rails and rested his hand on the curve of her hip.

Tangling her fingers in the fringe of his hair, Jen inhaled the scent of Old Spice and strong, healthy male. She'd always loved the way Zac smelled, no matter how hard he'd worked or good he looked. She gripped his collar and couldn't get enough of his kiss.

"Don't mean to interrupt."

Like a sharp syringe pointed the wrong way, Jen released Zac and backed up against fence. Heart pounding, she drew a breath and tried to steady her shaky hands. Tina stood beside her with a grin that could ignite embarrassment from a mile away.

"Nice you two are catching up on old times, but Patrick just called. He wants to know why he's serving a snack when the kids just had lunch?"

« CHAPTER FIFTEEN »

"HAVE YOU EATEN ANYTHING in the past 12 hours?" Dr. Jenkins studied his file.

"No."

"Anything besides water to drink?"

"No."

The doctor peered over the paperwork and pointed the eraser of his pencil at Zac. "Did you sleep well last night?"

"No."

Jen grinned at Zac's curt answers. For all his calm appearance to the world, she knew him well enough to recognize the stress steeped through every fiber of his being. Fear of the unknown brought even the strongest people to their knees. She'd done her best to distract him, but he continually snapped back to silence -- his way of dealing with what he couldn't control.

She stood beside Zac in the prep room. He sat on the bed in his hospital gown, his long legs dangling as he crossed his ankles. Holding his hand, she felt the tension in the more than occasional squeeze of his cold fingers. She tried to rub some warmth into them. No luck.

"As a show of solidarity, I haven't eaten anything since last night either." She peeked over Dr. Jenkins' paperwork as he made notes in his file.

"That's very good, Jennifer. You always were a thoughtful one." He stopped writing and looked at her. "We miss you around here. Are you coming back soon?"

"Not unless I have to," she teased. Jennifer smiled as the doctor stood with his back to the door, his white coat open revealing a dark blue shirt and a Garfield the Cat tie. "My plans for the camp are coming along great. I'll know in the next week or so whether my loan has been approved."

"Well, your plans sound exactly like what the kids need. Someplace safe to be a kid." He took his glasses off his nose and slipped them into his breast pocket. "You had a way of calming down our more fearful patients, they didn't seem as anxious when you were around. If you find being a camp director isn't for you, you can't always come back here."

She didn't see that as a possibility. "Thanks, Dr. Jenkins. I'll keep that in mind."

He nodded and turned to Zac. "The attendant will be here soon to take you to surgery. I know I've told you before, Zac, but just to recap, this is a very cautious procedure. We'll be under sterile conditions to avoid any and all contamination of the marrow. There can be complications, although extremely rare for the donor, the onus of complications lie with the recipient. I have your signed consent forms. Do you have any other questions?"

Zac cleared his throat, his voice obviously dry. "Will I be out for this?"

"Some doctors use local anesthesia, some general. I prefer a middle of the road "twilight" dose. You'll be alert during the procedure, but won't feel anything, but if you do, tell us. It's easier to come out of and afterwards, you won't remember a thing."

Zac nodded. Jen wanted to wrap her arms around him like she had her pediatric patients and reassure him everything would be fine. "I'll be beside you when you wake up, hopefully before you wake up."

Shaking his head, Dr. Jenkins offered Zac a kind smile. "It's not a lengthy procedure. We'll have you back in recovery in no time at all. Once we know you're stable, you're free to go home." He looked at Jen. "Are you driving back to Hawk Ridge this evening?"

"I think he'll rest better at home." She tugged on Zac's hand. "I promise to pull over and feed you if you're hungry."

Skepticism arched his brow. "That makes me feel better."

Dr. Jenkins nodded. "Zac, I'll see you on the other side of the procedure."

"I can't wait."

After the door closed behind the doctor, Zac released her hand and held his arms open to Jen. She slipped into his embrace, all her maternal instincts on high alert. "It'll be fine, Zac. I know it'll be a lot easier than stabilizing pneumonia."

"I was ten. I don't remember much of that." A catch in his voice belied his nonchalant dismissal. The winter he'd suffered pneumonia almost killed him. He held her tighter. "Is this really going to help, Jen?"

"It will." Jen scrambled for any encouragement she could think of. "This transplant of cells will give Carli a fighting chance. Once her blood cells begin to rejuvenate, she'll be on the up side of this battle."

"Doesn't she have to be here for this to happen?"

She brushed her fingers over the warm skin of his back between the edges of his gown. "In most cases, donors are found through the bone marrow registry - it's national - so more often than not, the donor and recipient are in different states."

"Mind boggling."

"The miracle of modern medicine. They extract bone marrow here, ice it down, put it on a plane and next thing you know, they'll be prepping the recipient for a transplant."

He sat silent a moment. "The recipient. That's all she is. Just doesn't seem right."

Before she could form the words to remind him Carli was more than just a patient, he hugged her close and blew a sharp breath. "I've come to terms with it. Everything you said was true. Neither of us could have raised a child when we were barely adults ourselves." He released her and instead reached for her hand. For the first time since the doctor left them alone, Zac met her gaze. "We're adults now. And I don't want to make the same mistake twice. We can still have children. We can do it right this time."

The depth of need so apparent in his dark eyes, her heart jumped and then settled back into an erratic rhythm. "Zac, we can talk about this after the procedure is over. Right now, we need to pray you through the next couple of hours."

"I've prayed for the last few days -- and not only about this transplant. God's giving us a second chance." Interlocking their fingers, he pulled her toward him. She reached down and steadied herself against his thigh, his firm muscles contoured beneath the hospital gown. "I can't believe it took me so long to tell you I love you. I want to say it all the time."

His lips pressed against hers and all the shame of her yesterdays melted away into the hope of today. There was hope...hope for all of them. She ran her fingers through his thick hair, her palm brushing against the smooth skin of his jaw. Their kiss deepened and all Jen wanted was for the day to be over and them on their way back home.

He trailed kisses across her cheek until he found a sensitive spot beneath her ear. The tingle that raced down her spine confused her as much as it comforted. Zac. Her Zac. Why was life so difficult to sort out when he was around? "Let's work on things one at a time, okay? First, we get through today and then we'll see what tomorrow brings."

People spoke just outside the door. The time had come. She started to break away when Zac tugged her back and captured her in another kiss. She melted. She stepped back just as the attendant opened the door.

"Mr. Davidson?" A slender, good-natured fellow with closely cropped blond hair stepped into the room. "Ready to go?"

Jen moved out of the way as Zac brought his feet up on the gurney, carefully tucking his hospital gown around him. The other man eased the covers over him and the blond locked the wheels in place. He smiled encouragement to Jennifer.

"He'll be back before you know it."

Jen grabbed Zac's hand as the bed began to move. She paced alongside, careful not to trip up the attendants. When they got to the double doors leading into Surgery, she pulled up close and gave a Zac a quick kiss.

"I'll be here when you got out."

"I'm counting on it."

The attendants pushed through the doors, leaving Jen standing and watching until the doors closed. She took a moment to gather her wits. Things were moving too fast. She never juggled priorities, but now she had so many emotions in the air, she didn't know what to grab first. She needed a couple of hours to grapple with her thoughts and bring order back into her toppled life.

Walking back to the cubicle, she grabbed her purse and headed toward the lounge area. Food. And coffee. Lots of coffee. She pushed the door open leading out of the prep area and turned the corner toward the vending machines. Footsteps clipped down the hallway behind her.

"Jennifer."

Jen turned. Grace and Martin Davidson walked toward her and behind them, her father.

"What's wrong? What happened?" Grace ran her hand down Jen's arm as her gaze locked with Jen's. "Are you okay? Where's Zac?"

Jen looked from Grace to Martin, and then glanced at her father. The grim set to his lips said it all. Ever since her mother had died, Jen knew he'd expected her to do the right thing and not distract him with poor behavior. All her careful planning...all her secrecy over her pregnancy...all the pain she'd bottled up inside herself just so he wouldn't be disappointed in her, now drained from her soul with the force of a tsunami.

"You weren't supposed to find out."

"Find out what?" Grace kept her serious gray eyes trained on Jen, completely crumbling Jen's last defenses. "Is Zac sick? Is that why he came to you? Because you're a nurse?"

Jen shook her head, moisture building in her eyes. She'd shouldn't be having this conversation with the Davidsons. Or her father. She wasn't prepared, and when she wasn't prepared for things, her words came out all wrong. *Please Lord, put the words in my mouth.*

"Your father got a call from a doctor here at the hospital saying Zac had been admitted." Martin said over Grace's shoulder. "He didn't say why."

Dad has friends in all the right places. She should have known something like this wouldn't be kept a secret for long.

"You're frightening me, Jennifer. Say something." Grace dug her fingers into Jen's forearm. "It's serious, isn't it? Some disease, right?" Her voice quaked as she drew a breath. "Why are you and Zac at the hospital in Denver? Why--"

"Zac is donating his bone marrow to a child who is suffering with a form of leukemia." The words blurted out of her. There was so much to say, she didn't know where to begin. "His DNA matched."

"That's why he was in the clinic in Hawk Ridge, right?" her father said quietly. "You'd been tested earlier."

"I wasn't a match." The tears pooled and slid down her cheek. "I wanted to be. I didn't want there to be any trouble over this."

Grace placed her hand over her heart as if the pressure might calm her. "Trouble? Why would you think there'd be trouble over trying to help someone?" She glanced at Jen's dad. "Who in Hawk Ridge needs a transplant, James?

He gave a slight shrug. "No one in town."

Martin frowned. "Then, who needs Zac's bone marrow?"

There was no way around it. The secret she'd been hiding for so many years couldn't be kept any longer. "Our daughter."

Grace stepped back. Martin turned to grasp the arm of a chair and sat down.

Her father simply closed his eyes and hung his head.

« CHAPTER SIXTEEN »

SHE SOUNDED SO FAR AWAY.

Zac focused on Jen's voice. He tried to tilt his head to the side, but it didn't make her words any clearer. Other sounds swam around him, or maybe they were voices, too. He didn't know. He didn't care.

He just wanted to find Jen.

His eyelids felt as if they'd been glued shut with rubber cement. A watery haze blurred his vision. He blinked until he recognized the swatch of denim fabric that dipped in and out of his vision. "Jen."

"I'm right here." Her fingers squeezed his. "Just like I said would be."

Silky blonde strands tickled his neck. Her nose brushed across his cheek as her breath warmed his cheek. The faint scent of citrus shampoo greeted him like a long lost friend. His best friend.

"Marry me." His raw throat rebelled against his voice. A coughing spasm gripped his chest as he tried to moisten his throat. Fisting his hand, he tried to lay still against the hacks.

"Take a sip." She slipped a hand beneath his head and supported him as she pressed a cup of water to his lips. "They had an issue come up and had to put you under. Nothing serious, but your throat will be a bit sore for a while." She let just enough of the liquid trickle into his mouth. The spasms stopped and his eyes opened wider, the haze gone.

Jen stood over him, her blue eyes bright in contrast to the darker circles beneath her lashes. Strands of her hair draped down to his cheek, swiping away the last of his fog. She was right, there was nothing to this donating bone marrow. He couldn't remember falling asleep. How long had be been out? He shifted to sit up.

"No, no, no, don't move." Her hand cupped his shoulder and held him still. "You'll get nauseated."

"Jen." He tested his vocal cords as he cleared his throat. "I feel fine."

"Good, because we have company."

Pain shot through his neck and head as he tried to move his head. His mother appeared beside Jennifer.

"Zac. Why didn't you tell us?" She controlled her voice when he winced at the tone. "We figured something was up, but nothing like this. We were worried sick that you'd contracted some disease."

His father cleared his throat on the other side of the bed, but Zac didn't dare move to look at him. "I can explain."

"I'm sure you can. Just like always." She tucked the blanket beneath him, her nervous energy needing an outlet. "At least you had Jennifer watching out for you. Like she always has."

Seemed like a good time to anchor himself in Jen's tired smile. The soft brush of her fingertips along the back of his neck dissipated his building tension. "It's just some tests."

She tapped his neck and nodded toward his mother. "They know."

"They know?" he echoed, the words settled on his mind, his fogged brain hindering immediate comprehension.

"About the transplant."

The transplant. Alarms went off in his head as he held his breath. He stared into Jen's smiling blue eyes and regrouping his thoughts. "Did it go okay?"

She nodded as blonde wisps of hair brushed her cheek. "Marrow all packed up and waiting for a flight to New York."

Tension drained from his shoulders. He wanted to kiss her. Tears burned behind his eyes as he blinked at the moisture.

"Jennifer was a tough one to crack, but having her cornered for a few hours worked to our advantage." Grace continued to pluck at his blanket. "A child. She had a child and gave it away. I can't imagine the pain."

"Grace, Martin, this was a long time ago--"

She waved away excuses. "You're a strong girl, but not that strong. No one should go through something like that alone."

"I wasn't alone, and it was a long time ago." Though Jen spoke her words softly, Zac knew it cost her more than she'd ever let on. She withdrew her comforting touch and backed away from the bed. She stopped at the door, a tight smile etched on her face.

"Since Zac's awake, I need to step out for a moment. I'll be back soon."

Zac wanted to hold her beside him, keep her near and offer her all the support he hadn't before. He wanted to tell her he loved her and wanted her forever, but she opened the hospital room door and disappeared before he could even grab for air.

"Are you feeling okay, Zac?" His mother squeezed his hand, her voice as gentle as it had been years ago when he'd fallen off his horse and she wanted to distract him while she checked for broken bones. Back then, he didn't recognize the tactic; now he knew she reserved that tone to keep all her fiercest worries at bay.

He needed to keep their conversation at a surface level until he understood what his parents knew. And his brain wasn't so foggy. "The doctor told me there was nothing to this surgery and he was right. Nothing but a headache and a catch in my back." He tried to straighten up until pain shot up his side. He stopped in mid-stretch.

"Don't move. Jennifer told us what to watch for," his dad's quiet voice commanded. Martin stepped up to the rail along the other side of his bed. He reached out and gripped Zac's forearm. "We would have supported your decision no matter what, you know. We love Jen as family. I wish you would have told us."

What was he supposed to say? She hadn't told him until a couple of weeks ago. "We were young. It was the course we were most comfortable with." As the words left his lips, Zac realized they were true. They had been kids back then. He'd made party-ing a graduate level challenge. For all the hurt and confusion he'd wallowed in over the past days, his bottom line reflected exactly what Jen had endured.

By herself. All alone.

"I know you and Jen gave this a lot of thought before taking such drastic action.' Grace drew a breath, the ragged edge of her emotions caught on her last word. "Both of you have good heads on your shoulders. I just hope it wasn't a decision you'll look back on and regret."

Zac looked from his mom to his dad. Strong, loving, Christian parents who never backed down from anything their three boys had thrown their way. They'd been there to support Nick when his wife died; they kept Gabe from working himself to death before Melanie came along. They took Jennifer and Kade in when their mother died and their father was too steeped in his own grief to realize his kids needed comfort and hugs. Grace and Martin Davidson understood the meaning of love. A gift Zac had always taken for granted.

Everything surrounding this operation forced him to look his life smack in the eye -- and he didn't like what he saw.

"Mom, Dad, forgive me." He glanced at both of them, the lines of love and worry a familiar sight. "There are a lot of things I've done that I'm not proud of, but loving Jennifer O'Reilly isn't one of them. Both of us have decisions to make over the next few weeks and I promise I'll share them with you. Jen and I have some things to discuss."

His dad patted his arm and winked. "So we heard."

The muted colors of the wallpaper calmed her mind as Jen walked along the corridor that led from patient rooms to the waiting area. She'd been taken off guard when they'd found her before Zac's surgery, but she was never surprised. Grace and Martin Davidson had an uncanny way of knowing *everything*. She shouldn't have been any more surprised to see her dad with them. After all, this was a hospital -- her dad's lifeblood.

The day surgery lobby was spacious and light. Plants of all leafy varieties broke up the sitting areas for privacy. At least as much privacy as one expected in a lobby area. She circled around one group of chairs and headed toward a back sitting area. She didn't want anyone to see her cry.

No one was supposed to find out about Carli. Then the letter came...she wasn't a match...Zac was. She'd wanted Carli to remain a secret forever, but secrets like this had a mind of their own. Okay, so Zac knew. She could live with that. But then Grace and Martin showed up. She'd never been good at lying. She had to tell them or have them worried sick over Zac and the procedure. But that wasn't the worst. The worst was...

She skirted a side table and headed toward the back of the waiting area. A man stood from his seat and held out his hands...

...Her father had found out. "Daddy."

Tears slipped down her face faster than she could swipe them away. He met her half way and wrapped her in a hug she didn't remember ever receiving from her dad. Sobs shook her, the force of her frustration knocking her off balance. But her dad held on tight until every last tear squeezed out.

"Feel better now, baby? You've been holding that in a long time." He patted her back with one loving hand as they stood there behind the potted palm. "I think you've held in those tears since your mother died."

"Daddy," she sniffed. "It hurts."

Sunshine poured in through the slated blinds. From the angle, Jen figured it was early afternoon. Seemed like forever ago they'd left Hawk Ridge, went through prep, the surgery and then recovery. Had it all happened in one day? Jen sagged against her dad, his strong arms supporting her leading her to the couch. She sat down and pushed her hair from eyes as her dad sat beside her. She'd been a nurse for years...some of those years spent working shifts in this very hospital. Why did everything feel so unreal?

"Jennifer, I'm sorry. I never meant to hurt you or your brother." Dad rested his wrist on his knee, flexing the muscles in his hand. "I'm the worst father ever put on this earth for not thinking about how your mother's death must of affected you. I won't make excuses or minimize it. Until this morning, I never even thought anything was wrong in your life."

You weren't supposed to know. I had everything under control. "I'm okay, Dad. Parents can't shield their kids from all the hurts in the world. You did your best."

"I didn't do anything except feel sorry for myself. What you've gone through...what you and Zac have gone through," his voice caught and he cleared his throat. "...is exactly what I'd hoped to protect you from. No matter which road you take, it isn't easy."

Confused by his sentiment, Jen tucked her chin and frowned. "What are you talking about?"

"Life. Life tends to repeat itself."

"Dad, I got pregnant and gave away my child. How does that compare to anything?"

A call for a Dr. Wilton came over for the intercom. Her dad glanced up and studied the ceiling. "Your mother was just a little older than you were when she got pregnant, only we got married. I was in my first year of practice and loved every moment of it. I loved your mother, too so I didn't think getting married would be much of change. After all, we spent every moment I wasn't at the hospital together. Money was so very tight, but we made it work."

"Dad, I never even gave Zac a chance."

His gaze roamed everywhere but at her. "When Kade was born, he was the most beautiful baby ever. Your mother spent every minute with him and caring for the house while I worked wicked hours at the hospital. I was trying to establish myself and provide for my family." His voice went low as if trying to figure out some question he'd contemplated a long time. "When she got pregnant again, I began to panic. Supporting a wife and baby, paying off school loans, and trying to help her as much as I could began to take its toll...we started to bicker. I passed it off as pregnancy instability for all of us."

"Hormones change a person, Dad. I wasn't very rational when I was pregnant." Rational was the last thing she was. She'd cried over cakes that burned, hot water in the shower...cold water in the shower, the lead in her pencil breaking. Anything that didn't follow her planned course had thrown her for a loop. She never showed her instability in class, but at home? Thankfully, Lisa had been a very patient person.

A slow shake of his head acknowledged her encouragement. "By the time you were born, I didn't have a compassionate bone left in me. There were too many things demanding my attention, so I evaluated them one at a time and decide the best thing for my family was to work and support your needs. I dove into work leaving your mother with all the other problems. God had mercy on her and gifted her with two great children. She never had a problem with you...it was me she didn't know how to deal with. My schedule was erratic, she could never count on my being home. When I was home, I was either sleeping or playing with you two. I never made time for my wife. After a while, she just gave up, she said she couldn't compete with a mistress that wasn't flesh and blood."

"I never heard her complain." Jen continued to grip her hands together, the entire revelation very unsettling to her. Her mother smiled all the time and always had time for her. She remembered her mom tucking her in bed and then sitting in the front room with a book waiting for dad to come home. "She adored you."

"She adored *you*." Her father was quick to correct. "Jennifer, your mother was a saint. You and Kade never wanted for love. She poured her life out on you. Me? You two accepted me and my absences because you never knew different. We looked like a happy family to everyone except Barb and myself." He drew a ragged breath. "She developed cancer when you were nine. That was the fight that drew every last ounce of life from both of us. Thankfully, the Lord didn't let her suffer. She died in her sleep."

The house had become empty. Cold and dark. Nothing she or Kade could do sparked any interest in her dad. "Dad, you grieved so hard. I was worried about you."

"Honey, I grieved over a relationship that never had a chance. When Grace Davidson scooped you and Kade up and told me not to worry about you and to go about making arrangements, it was like a weighty burden of dread had fallen off my shoulders. I didn't know what to do with you and Kade. All I knew was work." His laugh held no humor. "You stayed at the Circle D for so long I was worried that Grace and Martin would petition for custody. We all got back together at home and fell into a routine. Both you and your brother had found a second home at the Circle D and I wasn't going to rock the boat. I didn't want to."

She reached out and ran her palm over his forearm, the hairs soft over smooth skin. Nothing compared to the rugged strength of a rancher. Of Zac.

He placed his hand over hers and patted it. "It surprised the heck out of me that you wanted to go into nursing. I never thought you saw anything in your old man worth emulating."

I went into nursing to learn about cancer. I missed mom. I wanted to understand. I understand now. "You're a good father, Dad. I never asked for anything more." *From you...*

໐

Jen stood in the parking lot as parents arrived to pick up the tired campers. The late session of camp worked, but she'd have to gear it toward the heartier children since the nights had definitely gotten colder and the mornings were slow to warm. Hawk Ridge was beautiful in the fall, the fields golden as they surrounded the thousand pound bales of hay ready to be picked up. She grinned. Zac had done a great job as a hired hand. Maybe if he was tired of dollar signs and bank balances, he'd consider working for her.

The thought made her warm inside even as her joy dimmed. Zac wanted the Trails' End, too. He wasn't going to stoop to working for her if she was awarded the ranch. He'd probably never speak to her again. Stealing his dream was not going to endear her to him. Still, she'd never backed down from a fight. All her life, if she wanted something bad enough, she'd found a way to get it.

And with all his cockiness and bravado aside, she wanted Zac... she'd always wanted Zac. Talk about a lose-lose situation.

"Jennifer." A little girl with thin pigtails ran up to her. "Can I come back to camp next year?"

"You can come back anytime you want to, Carrie Ann." Jen smiled at the parents following their daughter, then focused back on the girl. "The Trails' End will always welcome you here, but I wouldn't be surprised if you were strong enough to take a vacation anywhere you wanted to by next summer. Did you tell your parents about the soccer game? You played the whole time."

"I did, Mom." She grabbed her mother's hand. "I played back field and even stopped the ball so the other team wouldn't get the goals. It was so much fun."

She intercepted the dad's concerned look. "We have special rules about playing soccer here at the ranch. There were no injuries, not even a bandage-worthy scratch."

Carrie Ann nodded. "Even the boys followed the rules. And Dad, Zac took us for a ride in his tractor. I got to stand behind him while he drove. The tractor was so big, I could see the whole world!"

"That sounds like quite an adventure, honey," he grabbed his daughter's hand. "We'll see how next year works out. Thank you, Jennifer, for the happy experience."

"My pleasure," she said as the family turned to walk away. The little girl clung to her parents' hands as she talked a mile a minute. Happiness welled up through Jennifer. This was her goal. Bring smiles to the faces of these brave children. She'd worked the pediatrics oncology floor at the hospital in Denver. She knew what these kids had survived. She wanted to offer them some small reward for the battles they'd endured, even if it was only spending a couple of weeks at her mountain camp.

"Ms. O'Reilly?"

Jennifer glanced over as an older man approached her. "Yes?"

"I want to thank you for putting the excitement back into my grandson." He pointed to a little boy helping his brother pack up a Lincoln Navigator parked in front of the boys' bunkhouse. "Mark didn't want to come to camp and now we're having a hard time convincing him to leave."

"Thank you for your kind words." Jen searched the aged face and saw true appreciation. "We try to show the kids they can do anything if they put their minds to it."

"Even dancing." The man laughed and shook his head. "Mark couldn't stop talking about how a real cowboy liked to dance. He figured if a cowboy who could rope a calf danced, it couldn't be that bad."

"He said that? I remember quite a different attitude from our Mr. Mark that night."

"C'mon, Ms. O'Reilly. Do you really think a twelve year old boy is going to admit to a room full of his peers that he actually liked doing something unmanly?"

Jen laughed. "I see your point." She offered her hand. "Please call me Jennifer. It was a pleasure having Mark with us."

He shook her hand. "Les Ralston. I'm always looking for ways to make this world a better place like the good Lord tells us to do. I'd like to sit down and talk to you about sponsoring scholarships for children to attend your camp. If you could put a smile like that on Mark's face, I want as many children as possible to experience the joy."

"I'd love to discuss the possibilities with you, Mr. Ralston." Jen looked down as he slipped his business card in her hand. Ralston Importers, Int'l. Lester Ralston, CEO. She managed to keep her eyes from growing wide. Trevor Hockett was always harping on her to find corporate sponsorships. How awesome to have one drop in her lap.

"Please call me Les. I understand you're in the process of purchasing this property at the moment. Smart move. You'll have a fine income base off the fields and I know you'll have little problem gathering sponsorships if I have anything to say about it. I'll have my assistant contact you in a month. We can discuss your plans." Les glanced over at the boys tossing a duffel bag into the back of the Navigator. "Right now, I'm just happy to be taking home a boy who thought he'd never see a reason to enjoy life again."

"I look forward to it, Les. And thank you."

Jen looked around the compound as kids hugged each other goodbye and parents climbed into cars ready for the drive home. She'd put in a long, hard summer, but she'd never been happier.

"That's the last of them." Patrick Marsh stepped up beside her and ran his hand through his hair. "Another fine summer at the Trails' End Ranch. What do you have to say for yourself?"

"I couldn't have done it without you, Patrick." She bumped him with her shoulder. "You've helped me so much over these two years, I wouldn't know how to make it without you."

"Sure you would. You were the one with all the orders. I just said, 'yes, ma'am,' and got out of your way."

She turned the business card over in her hand, allowing herself to believe her plan would soon become reality. Now she had at least one viable sponsorship to add to her business plan. Ralston Importers was huge. At least she knew they contributed heavily to the Stock Show in Denver. "I've got to tell Zac about this. If it hadn't been for his change of dance dynamics, I doubt Mr. Ralston would be as generous with his praise."

"Don't go giving that cowboy too much credit. You're the one that built this camp; he just managed to smooth out an activity or two." Waving to one little boy, Patrick then waved his hand across the compound. "You have a great staff to keep the kids safe and happy. I'm sure they all liked the riding and hiking and games, too. Oh, and don't forget the food--

you've got some of the best cooks around feeding the hungry mob."

"It took all of us, didn't it?" No way would she accept the praise he was showering her with. She knew it took a virtual city to help raise her village of sweet kids. Still, it felt good to hear that maybe she'd done something right.

« CHAPTER SEVENTEEN »

"How you feeling, cowboy?"

Zac looked up at the doorway from his pillowed recline against the cushioned arm. Sprawled out on the couch, a headache laid him low every time he tried to sit up so he'd acquiesced to building his incline one pillow at a time. "Like a load of rocks dumped on me." Her grin widened as Jen stepped into the den, a small box in her hands. "I'd offer to come help you with your package, but you'll probably be across the room by the time I roll off this couch."

"I see how this works." She set down her keys and the box and took off her jacket, hanging it on the peg beside the door before grabbing her things again. "Ahhh, chivalry. I really miss the days."

He turned on his side and made room for her beside him. "Chivalry has always been here, sweetheart. You just never looked for it."

She sat gingerly on the edge of the cushion with a frown on her face. "Grace said your back hurts. I don't want to make it worse."

"My back hurts because my mother won't let me get up and about. She thinks I'm going to bust my stitches. I told her I didn't get stitches, but she doesn't care. I can't wait for the explosion of Mt. St. Grace tomorrow when I tell her I've got a field to bale."

"Tomorrow? That's only three days after the surgery. Dr. Louis told me they'd bruised your muscles while extracting the marrow. I wouldn't push the activity if I were you."

She touched his shoulder with tentative fingers and Zac felt the heat flow through his veins that had nothing to do with the down comforter draped around him. He was tired of playing the helpful friend. He wanted to wrap his arms around Jen and hug her close. Of course, if he gave in to that desire, he probably would bust his Band-Aids. No use in proving his mother right. "Getting up and moving is the best thing for me, isn't it? You're the nurse. You should be nagging me to get up and walk around."

"I think you get nagged enough." She held out the box tied with string. "I come bearing gifts. A thank you for helping my last session go so well."

He recognized the Fred's take-out box and his mouth started to water. "How in the world did you fit a sixteen ounce rib-eye into a box this small?"

"If I brought you restaurant steak, Grace would kick me out on my take-out box." She untied the string, taking her time, making him sweat it out. If he could move, he'd have made short work of the process. But, since Jen brought it, she was in charge.

As always. "If memory serves, you'd haul logs ten miles by mule for a plate of Fred's bread pudding."

The aroma of cream, vanilla and cinnamon tangled together teasing him unmercifully. "Twenty miles and forget the mule."

Her laugh made up for her slowness. "It's not much, but I wanted to say thanks for all you've done, Zac."

His throat went dry. She didn't know the half of it. To have thought he wouldn't have helped a child after finding out he was a match hurt. He needed to tell her about the ranch too, and soon. Knowing the dreaded task ahead, the thought of biting into the sweet dessert turned to ash. He'd tackle the lesser injury first. "Jen, how could you think I wouldn't help my own flesh and blood?" He stopped short of calling Carli his daughter, though the word tried to roll off his tongue. "And not just because we're related. I think I would have done it for anyone who proved a match. This is life and death we're talking about." A funny look on her face slowed his tirade. "What?"

"I was talking about the camp, not the transplant." She reached out and smoothed his hair from his forehead, her fingertips lingering on his skin making him want to lean into her touch. "Zac Davidson, you truly are a man after God's heart."

He held the dessert between them feeling completely unworthy of any praise. "Oh, so we're back to chivalry."

Her intimate chuckle floated between them. "We're way beyond chivalry. You're so much more." She settled deeper onto the cushion and snuggled against his stomach as he lay on his side. "You're my hero, you always were. But that's beside the point. I wanted to say thanks for helping me with my budget and planning numbers. You saw how they perplexed me and just fixed it. I'll always be grateful for that."

His conscience attacked from every side. "Jen, that's what I do, remember? Create budgets and reports? It's the most exciting part about me. I don't see how you missed it."

Careful of his incisions, she rested her elbow on his knee, making herself perfectly at home in the curve of his body. When she chuckled again, he couldn't help notice how sweetly her lips curved up and how he wanted nothing more than to kiss her.

"So what do you call the impromptu dance number you played on my campers?" Her eyebrows rose, including him in her excitement. "Now that's exciting. They were talking about it all the way down the mountain."

"No way. Really?" He grinned, her exaggeration contagious. "All the way down the mountain?"

"It's probably legend by now." The tone of her voice heightened and her breath quickened. "I got my first corporate sponsorship possibility, Zac. Just like Trevor told me to do. Les Ralston wants to help the camp all because his grandson said a cowboy danced and made it look cool."

He saw her dreams blazing in her eyes as she chattered about the kids loving his choice of music, his dance steps, his roping and a couple of turns around the field in his tractor. Dust settled in his throat again. He had to tell her the ranch was no longer for sale. He needed to snatch away her most treasured desire and grind it into the ground all because of a clerical error. He'd made the deal right by Jess Eklund in a fair trade of investment bargaining. Making the deal right by Jennifer O'Reilly was going to be impossible.

Her fingers wove with his and she squeezed their palms together. "My prayers have been answered."

He stiffened, a flash of moisture lining his forehead. He didn't want to crush her -- now or ever. He wanted to hold her and protect her, all the things he should have done years ago. His fingers pressed her hand tightly to his. The way life ran, neither of their prayers were answered. Much like Grampa Jeb, Zac now knew what it felt like to lose everything. A hundred years later, there still were no winners.

Drawing her close, he savored the feel of her warmth beside him, her silky hair beneath his chin. As the Bible verse urged, he wasn't going to worry about tomorrow. Tomorrow would take care of itself. He hugged Jen close. Today, he'd bask in paradise.

"I'm glad everything is coming together, Jen." He nuzzled her cheek. "God has His ways."

Grace walked into the den, a plate of brownies in her hand. "Aren't we all lucky He's in charge." She frowned at the box on the coffee table, then her eyebrow hitched. "Jen brought you bread pudding from Fred's? I'll bet she's thinking of taking it back after hearing about the ranch."

A lead ball dropped in his stomach.

"No way, Grace. I came to celebrate. I'm so close to owning the Trails' End I can taste it." She nodded her head toward the treat box. "I thought I'd share the joy since Zac is mostly responsible for everything coming together."

Keen eyes shifted between Jen and Zac as Grace put her plate on the table. "She doesn't know? You said you were going to tell her."

Jen turned and looked at him. The idyllic thoughts he'd had exploded in a burst of broken dreams. He couldn't form the words as she eased back out of the circle of his arm.

"Isaac. Tell her."

He'd finally realized what true love was all about, and just as family tradition dictated, he gambled it away. "The Trails' End never belonged to the Eklunds." His voice sounded dim and far off. He cleared his throat as his mother glared at him to say the words. "I own it."

ⓐ

Goosebumps prickled her skin as the words cemented in her brain.

I own it.

All the warmth of moments ago, all the dreams she'd begun to think might come true now sat like a block of ice around her heart. She felt nothing.

"Jennifer," Grace began. "I don't know what to say. It came as a surprise to us all. Efrain Eklund never filed the papers--Gabe and Trevor Hockett researched the whole thing. They came up with nothing associating Eklund with the Trails' End, other than he paid the taxes."

A pain spiked in her head as she focused on Grace. "Trevor? He was in on it, too?" Her breath caught in her throat. "He knew about this?"

Zac palmed her shoulder. "No one was in on anything, Jen. The news didn't make sense to me when Frannie Pollard told me. Since I was going into the hospital, I asked Gabe and Trevor to run down the paper trail just to make sure."

Her heart began to pound as her stomach swirled. "Arthur and his father before him built the barn. They plowed the fields. They made the harvest." Her mouth tasted like glue as she moistened her lips. "They paid the taxes."

"Just because someone pays the taxes doesn't mean they own the place -- the taxes were never overdue." Zac's hoarse words crushed over her. "I was going to tell you, but the time wasn't right."

He tried to pull her closer. She shrugged off his arm and stood slowly, careful to stay grounded as the room spun. Was it all too good to be true? The harvest coming in; the camp's success; the offer of sponsorships. She should have known things were going too well.

She took a step forward and then another, and then another.

"Jen, wait," Zac called behind her. She kept walking.

Grace came up beside her. "Wait, honey, don't go yet. Please, sit down and let's figure out what to do."

Concern swam in Grace's gray eyes as Jen searched the face of the woman who'd picked up the pieces of her life so very long ago. She'd clung to Grace when she was scared and her father put patients and the hospital before her. She'd confided in Grace when she needed a mother's touch to lean on. She'd believed Grace when she held Jen close, rocking her and telling her everything would be okay. Jen swallowed hard and clung to that truth.

"Don't worry about me, I'll be okay." Jen heard her bright tone, but for the first time since she and Arthur conjured the dream--gave her hope for her future--she knew it wasn't true. Nothing would make it right. Zac owned the ranch she loved and wanted more than anything else. Zac wanted it, too. Nothing made sense to her, but Jen knew one thing--she wasn't going to let anyone see her fall apart. "I have to go."

Zac called after her, but Jen marched forward. If she didn't keep moving, she'd never get out and then everyone would see her unravel.

She climbed into her truck, flipped the key in the ignition where she'd left it and shifted into gear. As she rolled out of the Davidson compound, her fingers and hands tingled on the steering wheel as she headed home. Home. The cabin wasn't hers. She'd have to move back in with her dad for a bit. Not a problem, she reasoned, Dad liked her cooking. Thoughts ricocheted through her head the entire drive back to the Trails' End. The McMillan Ranch was still available, she'd have to look into that. Maybe tomorrow.

She blinked as she realized she'd parked beside the old stone ranch house. How did she get here? No matter. She killed the engine, left the keys in the ignition and followed her usual trail to the back door into the kitchen. Her vision blurred as she turned the knob. A tear escaped and ran down her cheek as she smelled the vanilla freshener mingling with the scent of wood trim and leather cushions.

"Why?" she choked over the word. Tears spilled over her lashes and wet her cheeks. "How could I work so hard and come so close...and then have everything taken away? The ranch; the house; the camp." Her fingertips brushed over the scarred oak table as she crossed the kitchen and into the living room. The dark pine floor, the overstuffed furniture, the massive stone fireplace swam in her blurred vision. She sucked in a stuttered breath as she sank into the worn cushions of the club chair and pulled the crocheted afghan over her.

Fresh tears blinded her. She squeezed her lids shut, rubbing her face in the soft comfort of the blanket. "Jesus, why is this happening? Why did Zac come back? Why did he make me care again? Why did Arthur and I create a dream that could never come true?" She pulled a fist full of tissues from the box on the end table. After blotting her eyes, she blew her nose and drew a deep breath as she tilted her head back and stared at the exposed beams lining the ceiling. Faces of all the recovering children she'd met over the summer filled her head. Their fears and worries etched on their young faces attesting to the fierce battles they'd fought through harsh treatments and medications, and the inevitable side effects that accompanied each. Childhoods eternally stolen by a despicable foe, from children whose only wish and prayer was to recover and be normal.

Normal. Her camp offered normal.

Jennifer drew a shaky breath as she continued to look up and study the roughhewn logs that comprised the ceiling, each timber shaved and fitted into place to provide a sturdy shelter against the mountain storms. Memories of countless snowy afternoons spent in the house talking with Arthur Eklund wove through thoughts of her mother, cancer survival and those lost to the disease. Arthur talked of his life spent in Hawk Ridge and the trials and joys of raising his family, and Jennifer listened.

She'd ramble about school, her years working oncology at the hospital, her aching heart for each family she'd consoled as their children endured vicious bouts of chemo.

She'd talk about her mother. And her father.

Arthur listened.

Come to me all who are weary and I will give you rest. My work is easy and my yoke light.

The words from the book of Matthew squeezed her heart. Wasn't that what she was doing? Laboring for the Lord, caring for His sheep? Her work for the Lord was easy, rewarding.

A chill ran down her arms and she wrapped the afghan tighter about her. She remembered the conversation she and Arthur had when she'd been accepted to medical school, changing course from nurse to doctor, to fight for a cure. The skin on her shoulder tingled as if Arthur's weathered hand still grasped her, his faded blue eyes boring into her with a strength she'd never encountered.

Why are you chasing after your father's dream and forsaking your own? The world has enough doctors. The world needs more compassionate hearts able to comfort the lives of the hurting, one child at a time.

The memory of his voice comforted her as if her old friend sat beside her, his simple presence and companionship her anchor in the tough decisions in life. Arthur had been there when she needed someone to talk to, to help her sort out life's choices. Arthur had been there for her.

Not her father.

Dr. James O'Reilly had tended others, caring for the pain and disease in the world, confident his own children could handle things for themselves.

And she had. She'd held it together her whole life all by herself.

She couldn't hold it together anymore. Her armor buckled and cracked. Her entire fortress crumbled around her.

"Lord, help me. What do I do?"

Come to me...

"I can't hold it together anymore, Lord." No more strength; no more fight.

Surrender...

A gust of wind blew from the north rattling the rafters of the old homestead. Jennifer buried deeper into the afghan, tucking her feet in the cushions of the chair. Tears flowing and her nose running, she begged forgiveness for...everything.

« CHAPTER EIGHTEEN »

"Looks like Nick'll be a contender at the National Finals Rodeo again this year."

Zac looked up as Gabe set his cup of coffee on the table and leaned back on the couch beside him. The pain in his back had gone numb and his head offered a dull throb as Zac picked up his daily routine. Nothing about his life at the Circle D had changed, only an aching loneliness strangled his heart. "Are you thinking about going to Las Vegas to watch? He'll have tickets if he's a contestant. If not, Cauldwell Cattle will since they provide stock for the NFR."

Gabe glanced over and studied him. "I think with your surgery, the twins coming, and all the unexpected surprises around here, I'll have enough excitement to keep me a good, long while."

"Guess you're right. Someone's got to keep a level head around here." Zac shifted and slumped back down on the couch. His oldest brother, Nick, dealt with the pain of losing his wife the only way he knew how...sitting on the back of two tons of angry bull and inciting its full rage by pressing his heels in its sides while it bucked an arena. Years later, he was still punishing himself. "Mom and Dad will want to go."

"What? And watch Nick get tossed like a yard dart from some brute of a bull? I think they'd rather hide out here and hold their breath in the comfort of their own home waiting for the call that he's been hurt."

"That's not showing much faith in him." An odd camaraderie filled his heart for his brother. "Nick knows how to ride a bull or he wouldn't be one of the top names."

"He's the oldest cowboy on the circuit, and for what? He doesn't need the glory; he doesn't need the money." Gabe linked his fingers together behind his head. "He can't keep running from your problems. We need him here, doing his part for Davidson Enterprises.

There were a lot of things he didn't need, but he did them anyway. "He'll come home when he's ready."

"Stubborn runs mighty deep in this family." Gabe shrugged and gave him the evil eye. "So what are you going to do?"

"About what?" Zac stopped his normal spiel in mid breath. No sense in hanging on to an illusion that no longer existed. "I'm going to talk some sense into Jennifer as soon as I can walk fast enough to keep up with her. She won't answer my calls. The two times I've stopped by the ranch, she hasn't been there. Her dad hasn't seen her either. She's avoiding me and that's a bad sign." What an understatement. He didn't have it in him to survive more her soul-gripping revelations. "Jen fights for what she wants."

Gabe lowered his arms and slid to the edge of the cushion. He squared Zac with a penetrating stare that only stable, logical Gabe could pull off. "How can you fight for something that's no long available? What's the point?"

"Just because we don't get what we want doesn't mean you give up trying some other way." He'd witnessed her crusading determination more times than he could count. "Especially Jen. I've seen that girl fight for causes that had nothing to do with her at times, but the injustice of it all sucked her in."

"Injustice," Gabe repeated. "How fitting."

"Come on, Gabe." Zac's hackles rose. "Don't put this on me. I was just as surprised as anyone to find out the Trails' End still belonged to the Davidson family. The courthouse made the ownership and deed right; I've made it right with Jess. Now I'm trying to make it right with Jennifer and she won't let me."

Gabe threw his hands in the air as if Zac had just uttered the most nonsensical thing he'd ever heard. "Jess never cared two bits for the ranch growing up. He's a money man, always after his next investment. You financed a business deal with him and that was all he was looking to get in the sale of the Trails' End."

Lowering his limbs, Gabe seemed to regained a bit of composure. "But Jen? Her heart's in that place. Remember the story about King David and Bathsheba? David could have had any woman in the kingdom. All Uriah had was Bathsheba. He was a faithful friend and loyal officer, he would have laid down his life for David. Instead, David took it all from him, including his life. David knew what he wanted and he stopped at nothing to get it." He skewered Zac with his dark stare. "You can have any ranch you want. Why take hers?"

Everything Zac knew about Jen crashed together in his mind. She'd seen no other way to give their child all she deserved - and allowed him to have all he wanted - unless she made the ultimate sacrifice by giving up her child. Pressure built behind his eyes. She'd lost her mother, she'd forfeited her daughter, she'd felt betrayed by him. "So you're saying I'm devious and ruthless?"

"Little brother." Gabe stood and looked down at Zac. "I know the Trails' End belongs to us, and no way am I arguing your assuming ownership of it. Deep down, you always believed the ranch belonged to us no matter who said what. But Arthur Eklund believed his ancestors, too. Great Grand Jeb lost it to Efrain in a bad poker hand. It's not Arthur's fault Eklund never filed the deed. Arthur made his offer to Jennifer in good faith. If I were you, I'd try and make it up to her."

"How?" his voice cracked, the strain of the last days wearing on him. "There are other ranches around here for sale. I've mentioned them to her, especially the McMillan place. It has everything she needs for her camp without the management headaches. She won't even listen. She's got a stubborn streak a mile wide. I'm trying to make it right."

"Maybe it's not the land she's looking for. Maybe she's looking for something entirely different."

The wheels spun in Zac's head as Gabe sighed and shrugged.

"Zac, for the sake of forever after." Gabe's voice dropped to that tone Zac knew well. "Are you going to choose right, or love?"

⊚

Slowing at the end of the row, Zac took a wide turn and followed another line of raked hay over the rutted ground. His back ached from the inflamed muscles from the marrow extraction, but a few pain killers kept the worst at bay. The main thing was getting the job done. If he stayed on task, he'd have this field finished by sundown. The entire ranch put up a day ahead of schedule.

Now that was something to smile about.

Are you going to choose right, or love?

His smile faded as Zac bounced on the seat of the tractor, Gabe's question an irritating burr on his conscience. What kind of question was that?

Right or love?

The ranch, or Jennifer?

Since the afternoon he and Gabe had talked, Zac couldn't shake the feeling that he was fighting a battle that no longer mattered. As a boy, Zac had stood firm in his belief that his great-grandfather might have been a lousy card player, but would never lose anything as important as a family legacy. As he grew older, Zac understood that gambling debts held merit, and by a miscalculation of face cards, GG Jeb had sacrificed a piece of his soul. A plot of acreage had changed hands, GG Jeb had lost his land and the other three brothers had been spurred into action, making certain that mistake could never happen again.

The remaining properties banded together creating the Circle D under a single deed.

Zac shifted gears and pressed the accelerator as shadows lengthened on the newly baled hay one row over. The whole field glowed as the sun inched down toward the towering pines along the fence line. The sun set quickly once it dipped behind the mountain peaks. Zac loved the night up here on the ranch. Countless stars covered the inky sky, something he'd sorely missed seeing when he lived in Denver. He looked forward to staring at the stars as he sat on the porch of the ranch house, just has he had the other evening with Jen. His chest constricted. Without Jen.

Tomorrow, she planned on turning her business plan on the ranch back to the bank, her long and arduous journey to ownership of the Trails' End over. She'd put up a good fight and came away with an extensive knowledge base of ranching. Once she got over the sting of losing, she'd see reason. She didn't need twenty-five hundred acres for her camp. If she wanted to stay in the Hawk Ridge area, there were any number of smaller spreads for sale and easier for her to manage. He'd always be around to help her.

Over the past few weeks, Jen had reclaimed that part of his heart that had always been hers. Being there for Jennifer O'Reilly was the most important thing in his life. He wouldn't fail her again.

He slowed at the end of the row and turned up the next, the sun to his back. After setting the tractor on course, Zac looked beyond the field and over the valley. Golden fields spread down the gentle slope, a series of lateral ditches criss-crossing the property making it look like a country quilt. The Trails' End Ranch offered a unique combination of hay field, grassy plateau, and forest rim. A grin stretched across his face. He'd wanted the Trails' End for so long, he couldn't believe it was truly his.

"GG Jeb, the Trails' End is back where she belongs," Zac said aloud over the low drone of the tractor engine.

The row ended leaving Zac only one more row to bale and the job would be done. Maneuvering into place, Zac squinted against the late afternoon sun. At the end of the field, a fence marked the boundary. He glanced above the three strands of wire to the rooftop of the old equipment shed, and off to the side, the barn. The angle of the sun reflected off the metal corrugation making the remodeled structure shine next to the log house a bit further up the incline.

The log house Jen had turned into a home.

He gripped the steering wheel and almost turned the tractor off course. The first day he'd stopped by the ranch house she'd been battling a broken water pipe...and losing. The house was old; it needed a remodel. Did she really want to tackle that? He could name any number of repairs the house needed.

As he brain tried to justify Jen's inability to fix one disaster after another, his heart reminded him of the day he'd walked into her kitchen. She'd sat at the table, maps spread across every horizontal inch of the room. He grinned at the memory of her juvenile reaction to her planting scheme. But to her credit, she'd sat and listened as he explained crop rotations and time lines. She'd asked questions; she wanted to learn. She'd trusted him to teach her.

He shook his head and popped back to reality. You didn't *learn* to farm on a place as big and complex as the Trails' End. The harvest was your livelihood, it paid the bills. One bad year and you'd be in a world of hurt.

Even as he fought to keep reality in the forefront, memories of Jen sitting on the porch in the moonlight filled his mind. Her hair a tousled mess as if she'd dozed off on the swing. He remembered her smile when she had invited him to join the kids for their dance night. The same evening they'd walked along the path as he saw her back to the house after the dance...where he'd kissed her goodnight.

The tractor jolted to a stop bringing Zac back to the hay field he was baling, and the tractor, and the fence he'd just run into. The metal post angled away from the left side of the engine, the top wires stretched so tightly, the two metal posts on either side angled in, too. Zac slapped steering wheel as he slammed the transmission into park and cut the engine. He scrubbed his hand down his face and stared at the broken fence.

Someday, Jen would thank him for taking this whole headache off her hands.

©

The manila folder dampened in her palm as she grabbed it off the bench seat and slid out of the truck. Why Mr. Gebhardt had called wanting her final numbers for the camp expenses, she couldn't fathom. But she had them, and they looked good. She worked her fingers back and forth along the worn paper edge as she ran through the final tally in her mind.

Four great summer sessions and one early fall session. All completely booked. Campers enrolled for next year. No matter how she looked at it, the camp looked great on paper. Too bad there was nothing that tied that success to the location of the Trails' End Ranch. She rounded the truck and followed the sidewalk to the bank. She should be happy the camp stood on its own merit with little of its success due to the terrain or buildings of the ranch.

Or the cowboy who owned it.

"Oh dear Lord, help me be strong," she whispered under her breath as she pushed the glass door and walked into the lobby area. Hawk Ridge Bank and Trust worked with all the farmers, ranchers and family in the area. Many of the elders of the town sat on the board. As a girl, she'd come to the bank with her mother to do whatever adults did at that time. Frannie Pollard had been the head teller and always slid a lollipop to her through the decorative iron rails. The smell of lemon polish on the old time teller counters evoked myriad memories, both good and bad.

"Good morning, Jennifer," Frannie greeted with a wide smile as Jen approached her desk. Frannie had gone from head teller to executive assistant and appeared to wear the position well. "Isn't it just beautiful for the end of September?"

"Glad the snow isn't flying yet. I still have a lot of things to clean up." Like the recreation hall, the barn, and move out of the house. Sadness edged over her. She had to move out of the house she'd cleaned and fixed and made her own. A house full of memories of friendship, laughter and love.

Just as quickly as the thoughts darkened around her, she shook them off. It was just a house. She'd find someplace else to call home. Her memories of Arthur's encouragement lived on in her heart along with the knowledge God had better things in mind for her. *Chin up, kiddo. It's in God's hands.* "And the aspens are gorgeous, don't you think?"

"Oh my, yes. With color like this, Hawk Ridge is sure to get folks coming up for some great pictures." She shuffled a couple of papers across her desk. "Maybe you can think about offering your camp facilities for camp dinners and hay rides. You've got the kitchen all set up, might as well use it."

A bit insensitive, even for Frannie. She didn't have the ranch, or the barn, or the kitchen. Again, she had to pull herself together. In a few minutes, the whole fiasco would be over. "Something to think about. Is Mr. Gebhardt available?"

"Oh, of course." Frannie stood and indicated Jen follow. "He said you'd be in."

The noise from the lobby faded as Jen stepped into the office. A pair of arm chairs sat in front of his honey oak desk, the seating arranged at angles for easy access. A lateral file of the same oak stretched behind a black leather chair, the same black leather matching the arm chairs. A desk pad, phone, and wooden letter holder occupied the top. A file folder sat on the desk pad, the only indication Mr. Gebhardt actually worked in the space. How did anyone keep an office that neat?

"Jennifer, come in," he greeted from behind his desk and indicated she take a seat. "Did you bring the final figures for the camp expenditures?"

She angled into one of the chairs and handed him the folder.

Opening her file, he thumbed through the papers, and then opened the other file and shuffled through additional pages. As he worked through the figures, Jennifer studied the brass mantel clock on the top shelf of the bookcase. It ticked a steady rhythm. Odd to hear a clock tick anymore. Mr. Gebhardt had probably searched forever for one just to rev up the drama of his loan procedures.

"Jennifer, you've developed an impressive business plan. Well thought out. Ambitious enough to demonstrate an understanding of agriculture. If you weren't a fine nurse already, I'd say you'd make a great farmer."

She smiled to be polite. She never would have accomplished it without Zac's help. His suggestions and foresight had put her over the top. The proposal was Zac's, not hers. "I appreciate your confidence. I guess the practice of putting together the business plan will help in whatever property I end up qualifying for."

"Hmm," he agreed. He pulled a page she recognized from her original application. "You included a schedule of equipment upgrades. Very good."

Zac again. "Thank you."

He closed the folder and shuffled it to the bottom of his pile. He tugged out a cover sheet she recognized as hospital stationary.

Her sponsorship.

He tilted his face up and down as he read the page, as if trying to find the sweet spot for distance in his bifocals. "The hospital recommends you highly for the Nurse Administrator position of the camp. They feel even though you're only a couple years into the program, you're well suited to this position."

Why did that matter to the bank? Still, she practically had to sit on her hands to keep from grabbing the letter to read for herself. The

Foundation was happy with her work. Now all she needed was a facility. "I'm happy to hear they'll back my work."

"Oh yes, and the accelerated program you've developed and tested has sparked interest. They'll be watching you closely. Good for you."

She didn't understand. She had nothing to watch. Only speculation, desire and dreams. This meeting had nothing to do with her present. And quite honestly, she had no idea where her future was going. So why drag out the pain?

She grabbed her purse, needing to get out before her tears embarrassed them both. "Thank you, Mr. Gebhardt. I appreciate all the help and time you've invested in me." She rose from her chair and extended her hand.

The banker looked at her over his glasses. "Sit down, Jennifer. You have some papers to sign."

More papers. For a failed attempt to capture her dream. The embarrassment was practically killing her. "I really do have to leave. I have a staff meeting--"

"Not before we finalize your loan." He placed a stack of papers in front of her and handed her a sleek, ball point pen. "I need you to sign all the highlighted areas."

A loan? For what? "I haven't researched any other sites, Mr. Gebhardt. I had to finish my year-end reports." She nodded toward the file he anchored beneath his elbow. "You've already pre-qualified my application amount. I haven't had time to look for other ranches."

He sat back in his seat and removed his glasses staring at her from beneath his frown. "You've changed your mind? This is an unexpected turn."

She glanced over the cover page recognizing her accepted dollar amount for the purchase of the Trails' End Ranch. Hadn't Zac told Mr. Gebhardt the Eklunds never owned the property? Tears stung her eyes at the additional blow to her ego. "The Trails' End isn't for sale. I'm surprised the Davidsons didn't tell you."

"They told me. And *it is* for sale. To you." He nodded at the paperwork. "Are you signing?"

"The Davidsons are selling it to me?" Conversations spun through her head. Grace's kind words; Arthur's echoed sentiments. "Zac won't let this happen."

He nudged her hand aside and flipped the first page over. "Isaac Davidson signed the papers this morning."

Zac's signature scrawled across the line. Nothing made sense. Jen fought to breathe around the lump in her throat as she sifted through the loan papers, verifying Zac's signature in all the proper places. She shook her head and pushed her chair back. "I...I've got to think. Excuse me."

Mr. Gebhardt stood. "Jennifer, do you want this property?"

"I don't know." Possibilities skipped through her mind like rice in a skillet. Why didn't this matter just close? She'd prayed and found peace with her decision. Her heart pounded in her chest and her hand began to tremble. She'd didn't have any tears left to shed; she didn't have the strength to fight anymore. "I'll be back."

She escaped the spacious office and ran past Frannie's desk, the secretary's voice floating confused congratulations behind her. Patrons lined up at the teller windows stared as she pushed open the massive glass front doors and stepped into the bright, crisp fall air. Trapped in a nightmare she couldn't seem to wake up from, she leaned back against the brick facade of the bank, squeezed her eyes and let the tears flow. Not again. She never cried. Since Zac Davidson crashed into her life again, all she seemed to do was cry.

Only a moment later, a familiar palm cupped her elbow. She eeked open an eye and saw Zac mere inches away. She closed her eyes again, sucked a breath and cried harder.

« CHAPTER NINETEEN »

Zac rubbed her elbow, unsure how to proceed. Not quite the tears of happiness he was expecting. He let his hand slide to her waist and tried to draw her close. "Jen. What's wrong? Talk to me."

Resisting his attempt at comfort, she dug around in her jacket and jeans while tears streamed down her face. Zac pulled a fast food napkin out of his pocket and handed it to her. She clutched the napkin in her fist and rubbed it across her eyes before blowing her nose. Lifting red rimmed eyes, she sniffed even as another tear squeezed out. "I'm finally okay with this whole thing. I've given it to God and everything will work out. Why are you dragging me into this again?"

"I don't know what you're talking about, but let's go to the park and discuss it." Wrapping his arm around her shoulders, he guided her across the street to same clump of trees they'd sat at when she first found out he had a back-up contract on the ranch. Ironically appropriate.

Wiping her face, she twisted out of his embrace and faced him her hands gripping his biceps. "Zac, listen to me. You've won. You've gotten everything you wanted...and deserve." With a quick squeeze, she dropped her hands and drew away. Hanging her head, she began to pace. "I didn't understand why the Trails' End was yanked out from under me, so God and I wrestled it out...you know, Jacob and the Angel style. I realized I wanted the Trails' End so badly, I never asked the Lord if that's what *He* wanted for me. All I saw was the camp and the kids. I wallowed in memories...alone" She stopped and sniffed, pushing her thick hair out of her face. "You know what I discovered? He wants the best for me and I have to follow where He leads."

"Of course you do." Nothing she said made sense. "That's all I want, too."

She stood beneath the aspen tree, its golden leaves brushed the top of her head making it look like even the tree wanted to offer comfort. "I've been alone ever since my mother died. I've tried to do it all and I just can't anymore." Fresh tears pooled in her eyes as she rubbed her nose and sniffed.

"No one ever asked you to be so strong." The magnitude of her revelation crumbled his heart. For years he'd imagined Jen as an impregnable fortress, a force to deal with. He'd ask the questions, she had the answers; he had the problems, she offered the solutions. Jennifer O'Reilly had life all figured out. Only, he had it all wrong, didn't he? She hadn't known any more about life than he did; she just made everyone think she did. Hoping maybe she needed him made him love her more. He reached out and smoothed wisps of hair from her cheek. "I want to help you."

She turned, refusing to look at him. The excited jabber of kids playing across the park floated around them. A breeze rustled the trees making a couple of leaves float to the ground. Zac inhaled the fading scent of sun-warmed pines soon to freeze when the snow began to fall. The worst winter he could remember didn't compare to the vast despair he saw on her face. "Jen--"

"I give up, Zac. I gave all my hopes and dreams to God and I know everything will be okay. I let go...of everything." She drew in an unsteady breath. "I'm examining my options."

A knot formed in his stomach. Was he too late? Had she already written him off? "What about me?"

Dipping her chin, her gaze followed the fallen leaves scattered about their feet. "You were the hardest to turn loose." Her voice so low he almost missed the words. "But I had to or I'd go crazy."

The knot in his gut began to unravel. This was his last chance to make up for all the hurt he'd caused her. He just hoped it was enough. "Jen, I know how much the Trails' End means to you. You've shared more history there with Eklund than I ever could have in my wildest imagination of GG Jeb." Her shoulders stiffened and he knew time was running out. "It's your ranch. The home of your camp. Just the way you have it."

He watched her chin quiver and the thought of more tears scared him to death. He stepped toward her and wrapped his arm around her, drawing her to his chest.

This time she didn't resist.

Holding her close, he wanted to hang on forever. "I've been a fool because I never thought anyone would take me seriously. But you always have, haven't you? You understood my dreams and sacrificed your own for them. I never meant to hurt you." He buried his nose in her hair, her sweet scent making him realize what he'd lost. "The Trails' End is yours."

"No, it's not. It's your family history, you love it."

His jaw brushed along hers, trailing kisses he couldn't stop. "I love you more."

ⓒ

She pulled back and finally met his gaze. He stood before her, no longer the little boy who'd been her best friend, nor the teenager she'd given her heart to so many years ago. This was Zac, the big, strong man with the killer smile. An irresistible blend of financial genius and easy-going cowboy. The man she'd never stop loving.

"The ranch is yours, Jennifer O'Reilly." He gave her a weak smile, uncertainty etched in his deep, brown eyes. "No strings attached. It will always be in your name and your possession."

She shook her head. "What will your family think if I run off with their property?"

His warm palms rubbed her arms as his gaze locked with hers. "It's not theirs; it's mine. And now it's yours."

Her heart pounded in her chest. Zac had always lived for the moment, rarely giving thought beyond his mercurial emotions. She wasn't going to let him throw away his dreams for her. She bit the corner of her bottom lip and let her forehead drop to his chest. "Zac..." His name escaped her lips on a surrendering sigh.

Strong arms tightened around her. His cheek brushed her hair as his breath tickled her ear. "Yes?"

Lord, I want this so much. I'm not strong enough. Another tear squeezed out as she clamped her lids together. "What about you?"

"Don't know. I could stay here." A note of longing in his voice. "Maybe go back to Denver."

Rubbing her nose on his chest, she tightened her arms around him. "Please, stay. Don't you see? I don't want the Trails' End." Her breath caught in her chest as she fought to keep the words back and losing the battle. "Not without you."

He kissed the rim of her ear. "Marry me, Jen. Make my world complete." Holding her close, he sunk his hand into her hair as his kisses trailed down her cheek. "I've been off kilter for a long time."

A fire ignited in her soul chasing away the cold that had surrounded her heart ever since she'd walked away from him so many years ago. This was real, she knew it. This was what she'd been waiting for and until the day she died, she'd give thanks to her awesome God of mercy and grace for giving her a second chance. She chuckled as she buried her face in his chest.

He stopped kissing her and drew back. "What's so funny?"

Straightening within his embrace, Jen looked into his gorgeous brown eyes and saw a love to match her own. "Zac, I've been holding on so hard, praying for things to turn out right. When I finally let go, God answered my prayers better than I ever would have dreamed." She leaned forward and touched her lips to his.

His lips claimed her with a hunger that sent a fire down to her toes. She snaked her arms around his waist and hooked her fingers into his belt loops, tugging him closer. He deepened their kiss making her heart pound until pressure built in her ears. She turned her head and he trailed kisses along her jaw until her laugh caused him to stop.

"What?" he asked, the rough hint of stubble sending tingles down her neck.

"We're causing a scene."

"I don't care." His fingers trailed along her collarbone. "So, will you?"

Goosebumps formed in the wake of his touch. "Hmm?"

"Marry me."

"I've never wanted anything more, Isaac Davidson, so yes, I'll marry you." She pushed back from his embrace and smoothed the wild ends of her hair in place. She couldn't contain an ornery smile. "But first, I should probably go back and sign my life away."

A slow grin traveled his lips as he fished a pen with the Circle D logo from the back pocket of his jeans. He handed it to her and claimed another slow, leisurely kiss. She melted in his embrace, returning his kiss with a slow, decisive claim of her own.

"Oh, yes, ma'am, you should," he whispered, trailing his mouth to the lobe of her ear. "To me...I'll throw the ranch in as a wedding gift."

THE END

Dear Reader:

Thank you for choosing **Second Chance Ranch**. Hawk Ridge, Colorado is a special place filled with special people. If you enjoyed Zac and Jennifer's story, please consider leaving a review.

Sign up for Audra Harders' newsletter at her website http://www.audraharders.com to be notified of her next release and for a chance to win a $25 Amazon gift card -- winner to be announced in the newsletter.

Don't miss her next release, the third book in the Circle D series, releasing in Spring 2015.

Discussion questions for Book Clubs:

When Zac left Hawk Ridge, he never planned to return, yet the opportunity of a lifetime lured him back and he realized that maybe home wasn't such a bad place after all. Have you ever yearned to get away from a situation, and then returned? How did you feel about it?

Jennifer faced a difficult decision as a teenager. How do you feel about her decision to give her child up for adoption?

When Jennifer was a child, her mother died. This event left a brutal scar on her soul, affecting much of her outlook on life. Have you experienced a loss so great it colored your perception of life for years to come?

When Zac was a teenager, he couldn't wait to leave Hawk Ridge and the shadow of his family. Why do you think he felt such a strong conviction to leave? How do you think his family, the small town, his own restlessness figured into his decision? Do you think he returned a wiser man?

If you were Zac or Jennifer, would be able to forgive the other for decisions made without the consent of the other?

Zac and Jennifer each have a deep, strong faith in God. How does their faith aid in healing their hearts?

Zac and Jennifer each had different reasons for wanting the Trails' End Ranch. Had the outcome been different, who do you think should own the ranch?

About Audra Harders

Award-winning author, Audra Harders, writes "rugged stories with heart" featuring cowboys who haven't a clue about relationships rescued by ladies who think they have all the answers. In real life, she's married to her own patient hero, has two adult children, and is surrounded by everything conducive to writing about farming, ranching and cowboys at her day job in the county Extension office. She began writing right after her son was born and sold her first book to Steeple Hill Love Inspired mere months before that same son graduated from high school. Surviving those years in-between reminds her God does have her plan for her life...and that He has a tremendous sense of humor.

You can visit her at www.AudraHarders.com. Readers and writers alike are invited to visit Seekerville, a group blog where Audra, along with twelve other inspirational authors, share wisdom and ideas about writing, life, and of course, food!

<<<<>>>>